D0866475

Daredevils

For Marissa, Danny, and Jonathan

—A. C.

A Peachtree Junior Publication

Published by
PEACHTREE PUBLISHERS
1700 Chattahoochee Avenue
Atlanta, Georgia 30318-2112

www.peachtree-online.com

Text © 2004 by Anne Capeci
Illustrations © 2004 by Paul Casale

All rights reserved. No part of this publication may be reproduced, stored in a retrieval system, or transmitted in any form or by any means—electronic, mechanical, photocopy, recording, or any other—except for brief quotations in printed reviews, without the prior permission of the publisher.

Book design by Loraine M. Joyner and Regina Dalton-Fischel
Composition by Melanie McMahon Ives

Manufactured in China
10 9 8 7 6 5 4 3 2 1
First Edition

ISBN 1-56145-**307-2**

Library of Congress Cataloging-in-Publication Data

Capeci, Anne.
  Daredevils / written by Anne Capeci ; illustrated by Paul Casale. -- 1st ed.
    p. cm. -- (The Cascade Mountain railroad mysteries ; no. 2)
  Summary: During the 1920s, Billy, Finn, and Dannie, living in a railroad workers camp in the Cascade Mountains, encounter Finn's air show pilot uncle, endure a troublemaking new boy, and stand up to smugglers.
  ISBN 1-56145-307-2
  [1. Smugglers--Fiction. 2. Uncles--Fiction. 3. Pilots--fiction. 4. Northwest, Pacific--History--20th century--Fiction. 5. Mystery and detective stories.]
I. Casale, Paul, ill. II. Title. II. Series: Capeci, Anne. Cascade Mountain railroad mysteries ; no. 2
PZ7.C17363Dar 2003
[Fic]--dc22   2003020622

CASCADE MOUNTAIN
2
RAILROAD MYSTERIES

Daredevils

ANNE CAPECI

PEACHTREE
ATLANTA

Central Islip Public Library
33 Hawthorne Avenue
Central Islip, NY 11722

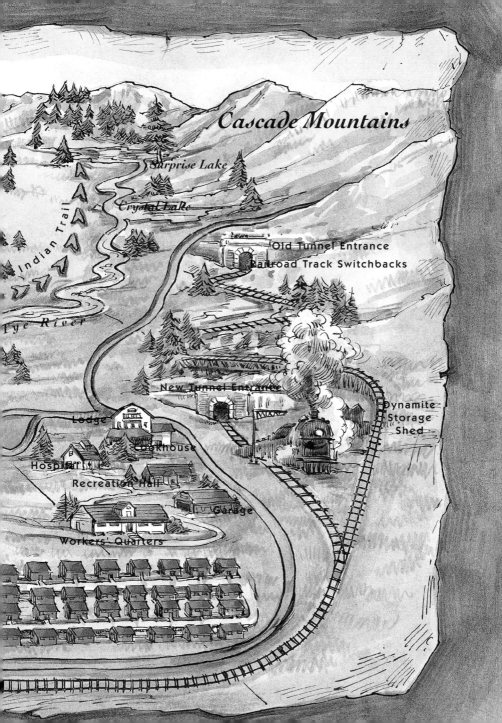

Acknowledgments

The author would like to thank the following people for their invaluable help in researching and preparing this book: David Conroy, Margaret Conroy Capeci, and Elizabeth (Buffy) Rempel for the wonderful stories and memories that made this series possible; Pete Conroy, for generously allowing the use of his photographs; Eva Anderson, author of *Rails Across the Cascades,* which provided wonderful historical information; Lisa Banim, for her expert guidance in helping to shape the story; and the Great Northern Railway Historical Society, for helping me to find detailed information about how the Cascade Tunnel was built.

Table of Contents

Chapter One
Something in the Air

Scenic, Washington
1926

B illy Cole had a knack for spitballs. No doubt about it. There wasn't a boy in Miss Wrigley's class who could make as fine a spitball as he could.

Of course, Billy and the other fourth graders were *supposed* to be studying their twelve times tables. But Miss Wrigley was clear across the room, working sums with the first-grade students. Sharp-eyed as she was, she didn't seem to notice when Billy pulled a piece of newspaper from his desk.

Billy had torn the scrap from his father's Wenatchee *Daily World* that morning. A headline caught his eye: "Crime Ring Smuggles Illegal Liquor into Washington State from Canada." No big news there.

The year was 1926. Buying, selling, making, and transporting liquor had been outlawed throughout the country by the National Prohibition Act. Many people were not happy about the new law. And many of them tried to break it.

Billy gazed at the piece of paper in his hand. It showed grainy photographs of two men in the crime ring. One of them had a wide face and a crooked nose. The other had sunken cheeks. And the beadiest eyes Billy had ever seen.

With a shiver, Billy tore off a corner of the paper and crumpled it. Then he put it in his mouth, and began to chew. Before long, it was soft and slimy. Just right. Billy rolled it into a pea-sized ball and slipped it into his shooter.

He was glad he sat in the back of the room. Just two seats behind his target, Alice Ann Lockhart. She, of course, was studying as hard as ever. Her head was bent over her math book. Billy aimed the shooter at the middle of her neat blond head.

"Careful," a voice whispered.

Billy glanced over his shoulder at the freckled face of his best pal, Finn Mackenzie. Finn's wild hair was so red it almost glowed. He nodded toward a dark-haired girl who shared the front desk with Alice Ann.

"Hit Dannie by mistake, and you'll be sorry," Finn said.

That was for sure, thought Billy. Dannie Renwick was the least girlish girl in all of Scenic. She could run and fish as well as any boy. And fight. She was smart, too. When a crate of dynamite had gone missing from camp a few weeks ago, Dannie had helped Billy and Finn find the thief. She'd also helped them find a hidden treasure of gold coins that had been stolen in a train robbery almost fifty years before. The three of them had been friends ever since.

Still, Billy had learned the hard way that it was best not to make Dannie mad. He took careful aim with his peashooter before blowing into it.

Thwipp!

The spitball hit the seat back just below Alice Ann's shoulder. Alice Ann didn't even notice, but Dannie did. When she saw the wad of paper, she flashed a wide smile at Billy.

"Class!" Miss Wrigley said, so suddenly that Billy jumped in his seat. He thrust his peashooter into the pocket of his knickers. He, Finn, and Dannie whirled guiltily to face front.

"I have an announcement to make," their teacher went on. "A new boy will be joining our class."

Phew! thought Billy. For once, he wasn't in hot water. Anyhow, he already knew about Philip Mackey.

Billy's father was the general manager of the Scenic camp. He was in charge of the crews that worked around the clock to blast a new railroad tunnel through the Cascade Mountains. If anyone important from the railroad company came to Scenic, Billy's dad was the first to know.

"Mr. Mackey will be here in camp for a few months," Miss Wrigley said. "And while he performs his duties for the Great Northern Railway, his son Philip will attend classes here."

"They're coming in on the train today," Dannie whispered over her shoulder to Billy and Finn. "That's what Mike said, and he ought to know." Dannie's older brother was working camp security.

Just then, Mr. Farnam stepped into the coatroom. He taught the older children in the schoolhouse's only other classroom. In his hand was the bell he rang at the beginning and end of school each day.

"Ready?" Mr. Farnam asked. He smiled at Miss Wrigley.

· Alice Ann and a few of the other girls giggled. Billy rolled his eyes. Those girls were always whispering about Miss Wrigley and Mr. Farnam. They were sure the teachers were sweet on each other. Billy really didn't care.

Mr. Farnam swung the bell. Both classrooms erupted in a clatter of books and voices and banging desktops. Billy dropped his arithmetic book in his desk and ran for the coatroom. He was just putting on his cap when Alice Ann tapped him on the back.

"You think you're so smart, Billy Cole," she said. "Well, you won't after I tell Miss Wrigley I found *this* on the back of my seat."

Smirking, Alice Ann held out Billy's spitball between two fingers. Then she turned back toward the class-room—and stopped.

"What's that?" she said, tilting her head.

Billy heard it, too. A strange, buzzing noise outside. "Sounds like an engine," he said. "And I think it's coming from the sky!"

Billy moved like lightning toward the door. Elbowing his way past two older boys, he burst outside and ran down the wooden steps. Boys and girls crowded out behind him, shouting excitedly.

Dannie's big red dog Buster was already in the yard. The dog kept barking and jumping into the air. It looked as if he were trying to catch whatever was making the noise.

Billy gazed up, shading his eyes. The craggy peaks of the Cascade Mountains and the towering Douglas fir trees hid much of the sky.

But the buzzing sound grew louder, until the air seemed to shake. Even Miss Wrigley and Mr. Farnam came out of the schoolhouse to see what was causing the racket.

"What in the world...?" said Miss Wrigley.

"It's an airplane!" Finn told her eagerly.

Billy had never seen a real airplane before. Now, like an enormous dragonfly, one came swooping over the mountains. It had two sets of wings and the propeller on its nose spun so fast it looked like a shadow.

The sight of the amazing flying machine dipping and turning in the clear blue sky left Billy breathless. As he watched, Billy saw the pilot reach out an arm.

"He's dropping something!" said Dannie.

A cloud of shiny white specks blew out beneath the plane. They fluttered and twirled in the breeze, sparkling like diamonds.

CHAPTER TWO

PHILIP

They're papers!" Alice Ann called out. "Hundreds of them!"

Billy blinked. As usual, Alice Ann was right. As the first fluttering sheets fell close enough to reach, he jumped on the fence and grabbed one.

"It's a handbill," he said, reading the fancy letters on the page. "For an air show. Right in Skykomish!"

"Elliston's Flying Circus," Dannie said, looking over his shoulder.

"Elliston? Are you sure?" Finn snatched a handbill from the ground. He looked hard at the advertisement. Then he let out a whistle. "Yep. It says here that the head of the flying circus is Ross Elliston. That's my uncle!" he said. "At least, I think it is."

Billy stared at Finn. "Your uncle can fly an airplane?" he asked.

"Sure," Finn said. "He flew in Europe during the Great War. Now he lives all over the place. Mother doesn't talk about him much. But I heard her say once that Uncle Ross was risking his neck with some flying show."

Billy read more of the handbill. "Jeepers. There's going to be wing-walking, loop the loop, parachute jumping... You can even go for a ride on an airplane." He grinned at Finn and Dannie. "We've all got to go!"

Finn bit his lip. "Mother might not like it," he said. "She doesn't think much of Uncle Ross. No one in her family does."

"Why ever not?" Dannie asked.

Finn shrugged uncomfortably. "Something happened back in Cedar Plains," he said. "That's where Mother's from. It was before I was old enough to remember. Must have been pretty bad, 'cause no one in the family will talk about it. All Mother will say is that we're better off without Uncle Ross. Truth is, I've never even met him."

"Well, this is your chance, Finn!" Billy said.

"Maybe," Finn said.

Alice Ann and half a dozen other children were already running along the Tye River toward the family cabins. They all clutched handbills. Billy was about to follow with Finn and Dannie, when he saw his father coming toward him.

"Dad!" Billy said, running up to meet him. "There's going to be an air show! Finn's uncle is in it! Can I go?"

"Hmm?" Mr. Cole barely seemed to notice the handbill Billy waved under his nose. Or the dozens of papers littering the school yard. Deep worry lines were drawn in his forehead. He pulled his watch from his pocket and opened it. "The Northern Express is due in soon, Billy. I want you to come with me to greet it," he said.

"But, Dad—" Billy began.

Mr. Cole raised an eyebrow at Billy's tousled hair and rumpled shirt and knickers. "Spruce yourself up a bit, son," he said. "Mr. Mackey's an important man. He's one of the owners of the Great Northern. Your mother would have a thing or two to say if she saw you looking such a mess."

Billy hurriedly tucked his shirttail into the waist of his knickers. "What about the air show? Can I go, Dad? Please?"

His father was busy checking his watch a second time. "Let's get a move on, son," he said.

Billy groaned. His father hadn't heard a word he'd said! Billy thought he knew why. His father had been working extra-long hours for weeks to get ready for

Mr. Mackey's visit. Every night, Billy's mother kept his dad's supper warm in the oven until long after Billy and his little sister, Marjorie, were in bed.

Billy shoved the handbill into his pocket, next to the peashooter. "Yes, sir," he said glumly. He shot an apologetic glance at Finn and Dannie. "Talk to you later, okay?" he told them.

"Not tonight," said Mr. Cole. "Mr. Mackey and Philip are having supper with us."

With that, he started back toward the main part of camp. Billy had no choice but to follow.

But Billy's thoughts were swirling. An air show—with Finn's own uncle! And a very mysterious uncle, at that.

"Our dynamite crew hit an underground stream this morning," his father said. "No one was hurt, but the flooding stopped work cold. We just finished pumping out the water."

So *that* was the reason his father sounded so serious, Billy thought. Men and machines pounded away in the tunnel every minute of every day. It was Mr. Cole's job to make sure the work crews stuck to a strict schedule. After all, he had promised to build the tunnel in just three years. Billy knew it was a promise his father intended to keep. Even a few hours' delay was a serious matter.

"I'm counting on you to help young Philip settle in all right," Mr. Cole went on. "The boy has spent his whole life in Chicago. It might be hard for him to get used to a mountain work camp like Scenic."

"I'll look out for him," Billy said.

That wouldn't be hard, he was sure. After all, he and the other boys in Scenic had come from far away, too. They had felt right at home in no time.

A jumble of buildings came into sight through the trees. Drill shops, bunkhouses, barns, hospital, recreation hall, cookhouse, and company store were all jammed together inside the curve of the railroad tracks. Tall evergreens grew close around. Billy heard the grinding of engines, pumps, and drills. The smells of diesel and dynamite hung in the air.

Up ahead was the Scenic depot. The wooden train platform stood next to the old lodge where Billy's father had his office. Iron rail tracks ran alongside the platform. Beyond them, the Cascade Mountains rose sharply upward.

Billy could just see the Northern Express through the trees above Scenic. It chugged slowly down the mountain toward the camp. Billy and his father reached the platform just as the train pulled in with a piercing blast of its whistle.

Mr. Cole walked to the very last car. Painted on the

door in gold was the mountain goat that was the symbol of the Great Northern Railway. The initials GNR were etched into the windows in swirling gold letters. A porter wearing a red jacket swung the door open. Billy followed his father inside.

"Jeepers!" he murmured.

Never in his life had he seen such a fancy railcar! Green velvet chairs stood on an Oriental carpet. An oil painting of a shiny black engine hung on the carved wooden walls. A crystal chandelier sparkled above a gleaming, polished table.

"Mr. Mackey, this is my son Billy," his father was saying.

A tall man with a mustache bent to shake Billy's hand. Next to him stood a blond-haired boy who was slightly taller than Billy.

He's a city kid, all right, Billy thought.

The boy wore a white sailor suit, polished shoes, and short pants. They were nothing like the rough-and-ready knickers and high-cut boots Billy and the other boys in Scenic wore. Philip's skin was pale, as if he didn't spend much time in the sun. He stared moodily out the window at the pine siding and tarpaper roofs of the buildings near the depot.

"Hello," Billy said. He stepped over to Philip and held out his hand. "I'm Billy Cole."

Philip frowned at Billy. He made no move to shake his hand. "This place is a dump. I don't know why Father dragged me here," he muttered.

"Um, what?" said Billy.

He looked uncertainly at his father. Mr. Cole was already talking to Philip's father about the new tunnel. Neither of them seemed to have heard Philip's rude remarks.

"Hey, Scenic's not so bad," Billy said. "Just different from Chicago, I guess. That's what my friend Dannie says. She's from Chicago, too. Anyhow, there's loads to do here. You'll see. I'll take you fishing."

"Why would I want to do that?" Philip said. "We've got lots better things to do in Chicago. But I suppose a nobody like you wouldn't know that."

Billy was steaming mad. "Now hold on!" he said. "You can't just…"

He clamped his mouth shut and relaxed his fingers from the fists they had formed.

You promised Dad, he reminded himself.

But now it looked like that promise might be hard to keep.

Chapter Three

STUNTMAN

"Come on, let's hurry!" Finn said to Billy and Dannie the next morning. "Quick, before Mother changes her mind about letting me go to the air show."

The three of them were heading toward the Scenic depot. Buster trotted next to Dannie. All along the road, children walked in chattering groups. Alice Ann and her best friends—Lucy Grinnell and Janet Kleig— skipped ahead. Wes Boyd walked with his big brother and a few older boys. Mothers in their better-than-everyday dresses carried picnic baskets and blankets.

"Your mother's not coming?" Dannie asked. When Finn shook his head, she blurted out, "But he's her own brother! What could he have done that was so bad?"

"Mother still won't say," Finn said. "But she's not too happy that I'll be anywhere near Uncle Ross. Made me swear not even to talk to him." He kicked at the gravel road, frowning. "The only reason she let me go is 'cause Mr. Mackey and Philip came to our cabin to invite me to ride to the air show with them."

"In their private railcar," Dannie said. Her eyes sparkled. "Just think, everyone in our whole school gets to go! Papa nearly jumped out of his skin when the Mackeys showed up at the door in their fancy clothes."

"Mr. Mackey wants to be sure Philip has friends in Scenic," Billy said. "That's what he told Mother and Dad, anyhow. But that snooty Philip is about as likable as a big, slimy slug."

All through supper the night before, Billy had listened to Philip's complaints. Philip didn't like the mud, the noisy machines, the smells, or anything else about Scenic.

Billy had tried to be nice. He even gave Philip his new cat's eye marble. But it made no difference. Philip said his pals in Chicago would laugh themselves crazy to see Billy's dumb knickers and boots. He even turned up his nose at Mrs. Cole's apple pie.

Mr. Mackey kept making excuses for his son. But

Billy could tell his parents were relieved when the Mackeys left.

"Maybe he's not as bad as he seems," Dannie said. "He could just be tired from the long trip or something."

Billy didn't think so. He had a bad feeling about Philip. A sharp whistle blasted. "Here comes the train!" Dannie cried.

The three of them reached the depot just as Mr. Mackey's railcar was being attached to the back of the train. Their classmates climbed on ahead of them. Lucy and Janet began exclaiming over the chandelier. Wes and some other boys ran around the velvet chairs.

"Boys!" Miss Wrigley warned sharply. "Mind your manners, please. We are Mr. Mackey's guests."

Mr. Mackey stood chatting with Miss Wrigley, Mr. Farnam, and Billy's father near a table with a fancy-looking vase on it.

Billy wasn't surprised to see Alice Ann standing right next to Philip. They looked like two peas in a pod— right down to the lace collars on their sailor shirts.

"I just know we're going to be friends," Alice Ann was saying. "I bet you're good at lessons, the same as I am."

"Of course," Philip told her.

The smug smile froze on his face when he saw Billy and his friends. He strode across the Oriental rug toward them.

"Who let that dog in?" he demanded, pointing at Buster.

Buster had climbed onto the car with them. Billy hadn't thought anything of it. Wherever Dannie went, Buster always followed.

"It's all right," Dannie said. She reached down to pet Buster. "He's with me."

"It's not all right," Philip said. "A dumb mutt does not belong here. Get it out. Now."

Billy couldn't believe what Philip did next. He shot his foot out and gave Buster a hard kick!

"Hey!" Dannie cried, as Buster yelped. She leaped at Philip, knocking him to the ground. "You leave my dog be! I'll teach you not to treat Buster like that—"

"Dannie, no!" Billy cried.

He and Finn dragged her away. But the damage was done. Miss Wrigley was already rushing toward them. Billy's father and Mr. Mackey were right behind her.

"She attacked me!" Philip shouted. He scrambled to his feet, red-faced and gasping.

"Daniella! How could you do such a thing?" Miss

Wrigley scolded. "Especially when Philip and his father have so generously invited us here."

Dannie's cheeks turned bright red. "But he—"

"All I did was say her dog can't come in here," Philip said. He looked at Miss Wrigley with wide, innocent eyes. Billy noticed he didn't mention a thing about kicking Buster.

"Apologize this instant, Daniella," said Miss Wrigley.

"He's the one who should apologize," Dannie shot back.

Mr. Cole frowned. "Philip is right," he said. "Buster will have to leave."

Dannie looked as if she'd been slapped. For a moment, she just stood there with her mouth open.

"Well, if Buster can't go, then I'm not going, either!" she said finally. "Come on, boy. Who needs to see a dumb air show anyway?"

Dannie took hold of Buster's collar and stormed from the Mackeys' car. Billy thought he saw tears in her eyes.

"But Dad!" he protested. "Finn's uncle is in the flying circus. We can't go without Dannie."

"I'm sorry, Billy, but we will have to," Mr. Cole said firmly. "Now, I want you and Finn to make sure Philip is making friends with some of the other children."

Finn and Billy looked at each other. Across the rail-car, Philip was talking to Miss Wrigley. Alice Ann, Lucy, Wes, Janet, and six or seven other kids crowded around him.

"Knock-knock," Finn whispered to Billy.

Billy had to smile. He and Finn had been telling knock-knock jokes since the first moment they had met.

"Who's there?" he whispered back.

"Ida," Finn said.

"Ida who?" Billy asked.

"Ida thought Dannie's the one who needs friends right now," said Finn. "Not that stuck-up Philip. You were right about him."

* * *

"Finn, look!" Billy said to his friend a short while later. They were pressed against the ropes that kept specta-tors at the edge of the air show field.

He pointed up. Three Curtiss Jenny biplanes were making wide loops in the sky overhead. They moved in perfect time with one another. But that wasn't what impressed Billy the most. He pointed to a man on the plane in the middle. He wore a bright-yellow flying costume. His scarf flapped wildly in the wind. And he was balanced on top of the upper wing of the middle plane—without holding on to anything!

Billy saw the big red letters "RFE" painted on the side of the plane.

"That's him!" Finn shouted excitedly. "My uncle—Ross Fitzgerald Elliston!"

Mr. Elliston's backseat co-pilot had taken control of the plane. It swooped and twirled above the enormous field on the outskirts of Skykomish. Dozens of roadsters and sedans stretched along the edge of the field. Hundreds of people sat watching on blankets, or stood behind the ropes in the spectator section.

Finn's uncle was doing the most breathtaking stunts Billy could imagine. For one terrifying instant, the plane hung upside-down—with Mr. Elliston on it! Everyone in the crowd gasped. Then the plane swooped down and around to complete the loop. Finn's uncle waved to the crowd from on top of the wing.

"Phew!" Finn let out his breath. He turned to Billy with wide eyes. "I thought for sure Uncle Ross was going to fall off!"

Billy hooted and clapped with everyone else. But he couldn't help thinking about Dannie.

"We ought to make Philip pay for making Dannie miss the show," he said to Finn.

"Who's missing it?" a familiar voice spoke up behind the boys.

Billy and Finn whirled around. Billy's mouth fell open when he saw Dannie. And Buster was with her.

"Oh, don't look so surprised," she said. "There's more than one way to travel, you know. Mr. Oliver over at the Scenic store brought us in his roadster. I sure wasn't going to let that spoiled bully Philip stop me from coming!"

Billy and Finn moved over to make room for her and Buster. Philip stood just a few feet away, with Alice Ann and some other boys and girls. Dannie stuck her tongue out at him. Then she turned her back. She, Finn, and Billy ignored Philip completely while they watched the rest of the air show.

"Hurrah!" Billy yelled when the Curtiss Jennys landed. Everyone else cheered, too.

The biplanes bumped across the ground. They rolled to a stop at the end of the field. As the pilots climbed from their cockpits and jumped to the ground, people swarmed toward them like hungry ants.

"Come on!" Billy tugged on Finn's sleeve. But Finn held back.

"I don't know." He gazed uncertainly across the field. A tent had been set up, and the pilots stood near it. One of them was a woman. She shook her long hair free from her aviator's cap.

But Finn just stared at the tall pilot in the bright yellow flying costume next to her. He was still frozen to the spot, unable to say a word.

CHAPTER FOUR

A DEADLY THREAT

Finn, go on!" Dannie urged. "This might be the only chance you ever have to meet your uncle," Dannie said.

Finn took a few steps. It was as if a magnet were pulling him toward the daring pilot. "I guess I could just look," he said. "That's not the same as talking to him."

The three friends took off running across the field. Buster ran next to them, barking excitedly. A stout, red-faced man was taking money from people who wanted to go for a ride in one of the biplanes.

Few people could afford the price—a dollar for every minute in the air. Those who didn't line up for rides crowded around the pilots. Billy, Finn, and Dannie squeezed past elbows and knees until they reached the front of the crowd.

"Sure, I flew during the war," Finn's uncle was saying. "Shot down my share of the enemy, too. First time was at the Bourlon Wood…"

Everyone around him listened, spellbound. Billy could understand why. There was something grand and exciting about Ross Elliston. He was tall and hand- some, like a hero straight out of a moving picture show. His eyes were blue, like Finn's. They sparkled with adventure. His thick dark hair had been tousled by the wind.

"M-Mr. Elliston?" Finn stammered.

Finn's uncle, still talking, didn't hear. "A German Fokker was gunning straight for me," he said to the crowd. "A mean-looking son-of-a-gun. But I got him, all right—"

"My goodness!" Miss Wrigley exclaimed. She stood at the front of the crowd with Mr. Farnam, Philip, and Alice Ann. "A daredevil pilot *and* a hero of the Great War. Is there no end to your accomplishments, Mr. Elliston?"

Billy saw the flush in Miss Wrigley's cheeks. And the frown that crossed Mr. Farnam's face when Ross smiled back at her.

"Mr. Elliston," Finn said, louder this time. "Uncle Ross!"

Ross turned to blink at Finn. "What did you call me, son?" he said.

"I...I'm your nephew," Finn said, stepping forward. "Rose Elliston is my mother. Except she's Rose Mackenzie now," he added quickly. "My name is Finn."

For a long moment, the handsome pilot just stared at Finn. Then a wide grin lit up his face. "Well, I'll be! And look at you—the spitting image of your mother." Ross glanced past Finn. "So where is Rose?"

"She, um...she couldn't make it," said Finn.

"Oh. I see." A shadow crossed Ross's face. Then he seemed to shake it off. "Well! You and I can get acquainted anyhow, can't we?"

Ross led Finn over to his plane. He ruffled Finn's hair while he spoke, smiling all the while.

"He doesn't seem like such a scoundrel," Dannie whispered to Billy. "He seems like a fine person. A hero even!"

She rubbed Buster behind his ears. When the dog trotted closer to Mr. Elliston's plane, Dannie and Billy followed.

"Don't you worry about your mother," Ross was telling Finn. "I don't guess anyone in the family has forgiven me for..."

He stopped in mid-sentence. "Well, they weren't too happy I ran off to fight in the war like I did," he said. "I got the itch to go. Guess I'm not the type to stay in one place."

Billy wanted to know what Finn's uncle had stopped himself from saying. Ross Elliston had run off to fight in the war? That wasn't so bad, was it? The man was a hero!

"Mr. Elliston?" Miss Wrigley said. She stepped over to Ross. "Seeing as you're Finn's uncle, well, would you consider visiting our school in Scenic? It would mean so much to the children."

"Oh, yes!" Finn said eagerly. "Won't you come, Uncle Ross?"

"Why, I'd be honored," the pilot said. He raised an eyebrow at Miss Wrigley. "But only if you'll agree to call me Ross."

Miss Wrigley's cheeks turned a deep red. "Well, I don't know…" She glanced back at the spectator section. Mr. Farnam was standing there with some of the older students. "I really must get back to my duties." She hurried away.

"Uncle Ross! What happened to your plane?" Finn exclaimed. He pointed at the bottom of the lower wing.

"Those look like bullet holes," Billy said.

"Afraid so," Ross said, nodding. "Got them when I helped the police nab a bank robber in Kansas. Cornered him in my Curtiss Jenny just last week."

"For real? Gee whiz!" said Finn.

Mr. Elliston laughed. "It was quite a chase! I..."

All of a sudden, the pilot's smile faded. His gaze had fallen on two men standing next to the air show tent. "I'll see you all later, kids," he said. "Finn, you tell your mother I'll stop in Scenic for a visit before me and the other pilots leave town. I might just visit that school of yours, too."

As Mr. Elliston walked toward the tent, Billy frowned. *I've seen those men before. I know I have,* he thought. *But...where?*

One of the men was much taller and heavier than the other. His beefy build reminded Billy of the mucking machines that hauled blasted rock from the tunnel. But it was the man's broad face and crooked nose that looked familiar.

Billy turned his attention to the second man. As soon as he glimpsed the man's beady eyes and sunken cheeks, he remembered.

"Finn," he said in a low voice. "Those men talking to your uncle. They were on the front page of the *Daily World*. They're smugglers!"

Chapter Five

WARNING

Smugglers?" Finn shot a worried look toward the air show tent. His uncle was shaking hands with the two strangers.

"What makes you think that, Billy?" Dannie asked.

"I saw their pictures," said Billy. He told his friends about the scrap of newspaper he had used to make spitballs.

"But what would men like that want with Uncle Ross?" Finn asked.

Billy shrugged. "Beats me," he said.

Ross and the two strangers stepped inside the tent. Finn frowned as the canvas flap swung shut, hiding them from sight.

"Well, I'm going to find out," he said. He strode toward the tent. Billy and Dannie scrambled to catch up to him.

"Those men could be dangerous, Finn!" said Billy nervously. Buster seemed to feel it, too. He barked, jumping around Dannie's legs.

"*Shhh!*" Finn hissed.

"You guys go ahead," Dannie whispered. "I'll keep Buster back here." She gave a low whistle as she ran away from the tent. "Come on, boy!" she called.

Buster went galloping after her. Billy and Finn were just a few feet from the tent now. Billy could hear voices inside.

"We want that cargo," said a voice that didn't belong to Mr. Elliston. It scraped against Billy's ears like sandpaper. "If the boss doesn't get it, things could get ugly."

The ice-cold sound of that voice made Billy stop in his tracks. Finn's mouth dropped open. He stood next to Billy without making a sound.

"Now, look here," Mr. Elliston began.

The other man didn't give him a chance to finish.

"Don't be stupid, Elliston. What happened to Lucky could happen to you," he said. "You'd better get the cargo to the boss soon...or you'll be sorry."

Finn's eyes were as big as silver dollars. "Those men are trying to get Uncle Ross mixed up in their dirty smuggling!" he whispered.

Billy nodded. He didn't know who Lucky was. But

he felt sure that Finn was right. "I bet they want him to fly liquor from Canada in his plane!" he said.

Billy took a step closer, trying to listen harder. But a strange grunting noise filled the air behind him. He couldn't hear Mr. Elliston's reply.

Billy turned and frowned. Some ten feet back, Philip Mackey was standing on one of the wheels of Mr. Elliston's plane. Philip pulled himself up the side of the plane, right into the cockpit.

"I've got to get him out of there," Billy whispered to Finn. "Before someone sees him!"

"Now?" Finn nodded at the tent. "But what about Uncle Ross?"

"I have to deal with Philip first," Billy said. "I'll be in hot water with Dad for sure if he gets himself into some kind of mess."

Billy shot a glance at the stout man who was taking money for airplane rides. He stood just on the other side of Mr. Elliston's plane. Billy hurried toward it, hoping the man wouldn't see him.

"Philip," he called softly, "you come out of there!"

"Make me," Philip said from inside the cockpit.

Billy couldn't see the railroad owner's son over the edge of the cockpit. He climbed on the wheel and peered over the side. "Hey! Don't touch those levers!"

Billy cried. "You'll be in a heap of trouble if—"

A large hand closed around Billy's arm.

"What's the idea, sonny?" a man's voice growled in his ear. "This ain't no place for kids."

Billy looked into the glaring eyes of the man who had been collecting money. The man's thick, sunburned neck was purple above the collar of his flannel shirt. He pulled Billy roughly from the wheel. Philip kicked and yelled when he, too, was dragged from the plane.

A crowd closed in around Billy and Philip. "Uncle Ross! My friends are in trouble," Billy heard Finn shout. "Come quick!"

Billy caught sight of his father and Mr. Mackey. Then Mr. Elliston came running up with Finn. The two strangers he had been talking to were nowhere in sight.

"What's all the fuss about?" Mr. Elliston demanded.

"Caught these boys inside your plane, Ross," the man explained. He shook Billy and Philip by the shoulders.

"Well, there's no real harm done, is there?" Mr. Mackey spoke up. "Boys will be boys, after all." He smiled at his son.

The railroad owner and Billy's father took Mr. Elliston and the red-faced man aside. Billy winced when he saw the dark frown on his father's face.

"Hey, Billy!" someone shouted. "What happened?" Dannie and Buster appeared through the crowd.

"None of your business," Philip said. He strode over to his father. "I want to go for a ride on the plane!" he said. He elbowed his way between the men. "It only costs a dollar a minute."

Billy's jaw dropped. He'd get the scolding of his life if he ever spoke to his father like that. He had a feeling his father thought a scolding was just what Philip deserved. Mr. Cole frowned again when Mr. Mackey took a thick wad of money from his billfold.

"Surely this will cover the price of a ride for my son and his friends," Mr. Mackey said. He smiled broadly and handed the pile of bills to Mr. Elliston. "And pay for any inconvenience."

The next thing Billy knew, Philip was dragging him over to Ross's plane. "We'll be the first ones to get a ride! You, me, and Finn," he said. He shot a smug glance at Dannie. "Dumb dogs aren't allowed on planes," he added. "Or their dumb owners, either."

Billy was glad Dannie was too far away to hear. "You take that back!" he said. But Philip and Finn had already climbed into the rear seat of Ross's Curtiss Jenny. Mr. Elliston helped Billy to scramble up, too. Then he climbed into the pilot's seat.

"Uncle Ross? What did those men want?" Finn asked. He pointed toward the long line of automobiles at the edge of the field.

The two men his uncle had been talking to were getting into a black sedan. Mr. Elliston glanced at them as he put on his aviator's cap and glasses.

"Oh, nothing much," he said.

"Well, I don't like them," Finn said, scowling. "We heard what they said! Something about the boss. And some kind of cargo they want you to get. It sounded like rough business, Uncle Ross."

"Sounded like bootlegging, that's what," Billy added.

The pilot's eyes darted from Finn to Billy. Then he chuckled. "Now don't you boys go jumping to conclusions. Things aren't always the way they seem," he said. "That was nothing to worry about. Nothing at all."

Billy wondered how Mr. Elliston could be so sure. But he didn't have a chance to ask.

"Hey! My father is paying you to fly, not talk," Philip said. He banged on the cockpit with his fist.

Billy groaned. Why did Philip always butt in and ruin everything? Mr. Elliston didn't seem to mind, though. He winked at Billy and Finn.

"Okay, boys," he said. "Let's fly!"

The engine started with a roar. A moment later, the plane bumped forward over the ground. Faster and faster it went, shaking wildly. Billy felt sure his teeth would crack from so much banging together.

Then, suddenly, it happened. The great, metal nose of the plane lifted up, and the shaking stopped. They were in the air! Billy felt weightless. The wind flattened his cheeks. Higher and higher they went. Billy peered over the side of the cockpit, and a thrill shot through him.

"Finn, look!" he shouted.

All of Skykomish spread out below them. The field looked like an enormous rectangle of green. People and automobiles were splashes of color moving across it. Billy saw the stores along Main Street and houses among the trees beyond. He saw the steep roof of the Skykomish train depot. Gleaming rails curved away from it in both directions.

"We can see everything!" Billy said. He pointed at a tarp next to the train tracks that ran through the woods. A dark triangle was visible on a crate that stuck out from beneath the tarp. "You can even make out the marks on that pile of supplies! Guess some work crew is going to be fixing the tracks."

"Who cares? I want to go higher!" Philip shouted over the roaring engine.

Finn said nothing. A slight frown stayed on his face until after the plane landed, about ten minutes later. His uncle seemed to notice it, too.

"About those fellows," Mr. Elliston said, as he helped Finn to climb down from the plane. "What do you say we keep that just between us? I sure wouldn't want your mother to get the wrong idea. She already thinks I'm a bad sort."

"But you didn't do anything wrong, Uncle Ross," Finn said. He looked sideways at Philip, then lowered his voice. "Those men made threats! What if they try to cause trouble for you?"

Mr. Elliston reached out to ruffle Billy's hair. "Don't you worry, son. They won't hurt me," he said. Behind him, the red-faced man was hustling two young men over to the Curtiss Jenny. "Remember, I'll stop by Scenic to see your family. Day after tomorrow, all right? And you tell that pretty teacher of yours I'll be there to visit your class, too. Right after lunch."

* * *

"I'll be giving Mr. Mackey and Philip a tour of the tunnel this afternoon," Mr. Cole said at breakfast Monday morning. He gazed at Billy over his plate of fried eggs and sausages. "I want you to come with us."

Billy looked up from the funny pages that lay on the table next to his plate. "Today? But Finn's uncle is visiting the school this afternoon!" he said.

"I've already talked to your teacher," his father said. "That pilot fellow will be coming with you and Philip. Miss Wrigley agreed to send the three of you to the tunnel at two o'clock."

"Not Finn?" Billy asked, disappointed.

Mr. Cole shook his head. "Finn's mother and father don't want him to miss any lessons," he said.

Billy wondered if Mr. and Mrs. Mackenzie had a different reason. Could it be they still didn't want Finn to spend time with Uncle Ross?

"Can I go?" asked Billy's five-year-old sister. As usual, Marjorie had eaten only the whites of her eggs. The fried yolks, with their nibbled edges, were growing cold on her plate.

"Certainly not," Mrs. Cole said firmly. "I even have my doubts about letting Billy go." She turned to Billy's father. "Do you think it's safe?"

"There's nothing to worry about. The water's been pumped out of the tunnel," Mr. Cole said. "I'll admit, Mackey spoils that boy of his rotten. But if he wants Philip along, then I think Billy ought to be there, too."

The *Daily World* was on the table. Billy's father seemed too distracted to read it. He stood up to go, leaving the paper where it was.

"How's Philip settling in, Billy?" he asked. "Is he making friends all right?"

Chapter Six

BAD LUCK

Billy's stomach churned all morning long. He couldn't stop thinking about Lucky Larry, lying cold in the Seattle shipyards. And he couldn't stop worrying about Finn's uncle.

What if Mr. Elliston's luck ran out, just as Lucky Larry's had?

Miss Wrigley was already leading the class in the morning prayer when Billy got to school. He didn't have a chance to talk to Finn and Dannie until noontime recess. *After* he wiped the blackboard to make up for being tardy. By the time he got outside, Billy was ready to burst with his news.

"Finn! Dannie!" he called.

He ran past the younger boys and girls who sat on the school steps. Finn and Dannie were eating lunch along the riverbank with the older children. They cheered as Eddie Boyd and Jim Walsh played chicken on a tree trunk that had fallen across the river. The two boys tugged and pushed at each other. Billy barely glanced at them.

"Look at this!" he said. He dropped down next to Dannie and Finn on the soft pine needles. Billy reached into his lunch pail. He pulled out the article he had ripped from the newspaper. Finn's eyes got wider and wider as he read it.

"Looks like those men we saw with Uncle Ross *are* smugglers!" he said. "And maybe murderers, too!"

"I reckon so," Billy said. "They did say Ross could end up like Lucky, remember? And now we know Lucky was killed. He went against the crime ring and talked to police!"

"So they might go after your uncle, too, if he won't smuggle bootleg liquor for them in his plane." Dannie pounded a fist against the ground. "It isn't fair! Isn't there something we can do to stop them?"

Another cheer rose around them. Billy looked up in time to see Eddie push Jim off balance on the log. Jim fell into the knee-deep river with a splash. Water sprayed over Finn, Dannie, and Billy.

"Ha!" said Alice Ann. She, Lucy, and Janet sat with Philip a few feet away. "That's what you get for thinking you can outwit a whole gang of bootleg smugglers."

Billy hadn't realized she was listening to them. Alice Ann turned to Philip with her nose in the air. "Those three think they're better than the police even," she said. "Just because they found some missing gold a while back."

"Those know-nothings?" Philip laughed. "They couldn't outsmart a worm!"

"Oh yeah?" Dannie jumped to her feet. She raced down the riverbank and climbed onto the empty log. "You think you're better than me?" she said, pointing at Philip. "Come up here and prove it! I dare you!"

"I, um..." Philip glanced around uncertainly. "I don't need to play a dumb game to show I'm better than you," he said.

Still, he looked relieved when Miss Wrigley appeared on the schoolhouse steps to call them in. Philip scrambled away without looking at Dannie.

Ordinarily, Finn was one of the last to return to the classroom after lunch. Today, he was the first. He practically dragged Billy and Dannie up the steps.

"We've got to talk to Uncle Ross about those men," Finn said, as they sat at their desks. "How could he tell us there's nothing to worry about? Doesn't he know what happened to Lucky Larry?"

"Come to order, class!" Miss Wrigley said, clapping her hands.

Billy noticed that their teacher seemed to have even more energy than usual. She darted all over, straightening desks and papers. When Mr. Elliston arrived, she was standing on her chair, hanging the flag in a new spot over the blackboard.

"Miss Wrigley?" The handsome pilot stood in the doorway with his hat in his hand. He wore a smart-looking jacket buttoned over a vest and tie.

"Oh!" Miss Wrigley stepped quickly down, smoothing her skirt. Her cheeks were pink as she hurried to shake hands with her guest. "Thank you so much for coming, Mr. Elliston."

"I thought we agreed you would call me Ross," Finn's uncle said.

Miss Wrigley's cheeks turned bright red. Billy had never heard her call any of the men in camp by their first name. He guessed it had something to do with the "proper manners" his mother talked about sometimes.

"I, er... Excuse me, I'll be right back," Miss Wrigley said. "Children, I want you all to work on your lessons." Flustered, she stepped into the coatroom to call Mr. Farnam's class.

The moment she was gone, Finn jumped up from his

desk. He grabbed Billy and pulled him over to Mr. Elliston while their classmates began to do sums. "Well hello, boys!" Finn's uncle said. A broad smile spread across his face. "Say, Finn. Why don't we go visit your mother when we're done here?"

Finn squirmed uncomfortably. "Um… Don't you want to see the tunnel, Uncle Ross?" he said. "A whole tour's already been set up."

The pilot looked hard at Finn. "Rose still won't see me, eh?" he said.

"No, sir," Finn said quietly. "She won't let me go on the tour with you, either. Sorry, Uncle Ross."

Billy felt bad for Finn and his uncle. He nudged Finn with his elbow. "What about those two men?" he whispered.

Mr. Elliston raised an eyebrow. "What men?"

"The ones we saw yesterday!" said Finn. "You told us not to worry about them. But those men *kill* people who don't do what they want."

Billy showed Finn's uncle the newspaper clipping about the government raid. As he read, a frown wrinkled his brow.

"Ross Elliston doesn't take orders from no-good smugglers," he said. "It's a shame, what happened to that Larry fellow. But those men won't touch me. Just let them try! I wasn't afraid to fly against a dozen German Fokkers at Meuse. I'm sure not going to let a couple of nickel hoodlums scare me now."

Just then, Miss Wrigley hurried back into the room. Mr. Farnam was behind her with his class of older boys and girls. He shook Mr. Elliston's hand, but his smile wasn't welcoming.

"Are you treating the children to your wartime stories already, Mr. Elliston?" Miss Wrigley asked. "I mean, Ross," she added.

Mr. Farnam frowned. "Boys, please take your seats," he told Billy and Finn.

They sat down. But Billy couldn't stop thinking about the two men who had threatened Ross at the air show. He wanted to believe those men would leave Finn's uncle alone. But then he pictured the shorter man's beady eyes, and the larger man's huge, square body.

And the cold knot in his gut twisted tighter and tighter.

* * *

At two o'clock, Billy and Philip left the schoolhouse with Mr. Elliston. Finn and Dannie looked as if they were itching to come along.

Too bad they can't come instead of Philip, Billy thought.

But he was stuck with the railroad owner's son. And so was Finn's uncle. Philip pestered Mr. Elliston with his bragging and questions while they walked across camp. He didn't stop jabbering until they reached the tunnel. Mr. Elliston winked at Billy behind Philip's back.

Billy saw an engine outside the tunnel entrance. A single, open work car was hitched to it. It was the same kind that carried men to their shifts inside the tunnel. Billy's father and Mr. Mackey were already sitting on two of the seats. Ross, Billy, and Philip quickly joined them. Once they were on board, Dannie's older brother Mike hopped into the rear of the car. He wore an armband pinned to his shirt. The word SECURITY was printed on it.

Mr. Cole signaled the engineer, and the small train lurched forward. Ross peered into the murky darkness inside the tunnel.

"Well, now!" he said. "I'm used to the skies. But this is the first time I've been inside a mountain."

As the work car moved out of the sunlight, the air grew cool and moist. Goosebumps popped out on Billy's arms. He smelled oil and rock, and the sharp scent of dynamite. Electric lamps on the sides of the car lit the roughly blasted rock around them.

"Our crews have already broken records for the most drilling in thirty days' time," Billy's father told Mr. Mackey proudly. "They're averaging five rounds a day. The tunnel moves forward eight feet with each round. Our mucking machines can load fifty cubic feet of blasted rock onto a car in just three minutes."

Mr. Mackey nodded. Billy saw the way his eyes took in every detail. "At this rate, we might even hole through the mountain ahead of schedule," Mr. Mackey said.

Billy's father didn't usually show his feelings much. But Billy saw a smile flicker over his face. Mr. Cole nodded ahead at a faint light deep inside the tunnel. "That engine heading toward us is bringing a load of granite out right now," he said.

As the engine neared, the screeching of wheels against the tracks was deafening. Billy had to cover his ears. At last the cars came rumbling past, piled high with chunks of grimy granite.

"Look! A rock fell out!" Philip shouted over the din. He leaned over the side of the car. "I'm going to get it."

"What?" Mike said. He shook his head. "You can't do that! It's dangerous."

Philip ignored him. "Stop the car!" he ordered.

Billy's father frowned in the yellow glow from the lamps. "You'd best stay here, young man," he said.

"Now, son," Mr. Mackey began. "I really don't think you should…"

But Philip didn't wait for his father to finish. He jumped right off the slowly moving train—and stumbled onto the opposite tracks.

"Philip!" Mr. Mackey called in alarm.

The work car ground to a halt. Frowning, Mike jumped over the side of the car. He grabbed Philip's arm and stopped.

"What's that?" Mike said. He stared deeper into the tunnel.

Billy heard something, too. Shouting. And another sound. A rumbling *whoosh* that made his hair stand on end.

"Water," Mr. Cole said. His face turned pale. "The men must have hit another underground stream. Everyone inside the tunnel is in danger. Philip, get back on here. Now!"

"Not until I get my rock," Philip insisted.

"Philip!" Mr. Mackey started to climb down to the tracks, but Mr. Elliston beat him to it. He jumped over the side of the car and helped Mike pull Philip back.

They tried to, anyway. Philip fought against them, trying to reach the chunk of granite. Mike and Ross kept glancing nervously over their shoulders.

The sounds of rushing water grew louder. Billy gulped.

This wasn't just an underground stream. It was a wall of water.

And it was roaring straight toward them!

CHAPTER SEVEN
DISASTER IN THE TUNNEL

Billy clutched the side of the work car. There was nowhere to go. The water would hit at any second.

"Help!" Philip yelled over the deafening roar.

Mike and Mr. Elliston pushed Philip along, trying not to get kicked by his flailing legs. Gasping, Philip fell into the car.

"Hurry!" Mr. Cole leaned over the side and reached for Mike's hand.

Bam!

The wall of water slammed into the engine and work car. The train lurched sideways. With a metallic screech, it crashed into the solid granite of the tunnel wall. Water pounded against Billy. It threw him off the seat and filled his nose and mouth.

Terror shot through him. He was going to drown!

Trapped in the rushing water, Billy had no idea which direction was up.

Then his hand hit a metal railing. He grabbed it and held on for his life. At least he was still inside the work train.

Water gushed past, as high as the top of the car. Billy's shoulders ached from struggling against the powerful current.

"Dad!" he gasped. "Where are you?"

"I'm all right, son!" Mr. Cole's called above the roar of the water. "Hang on. It'll ease up in a minute. The worst is over now."

Billy saw his father's head and shoulders above the water at the other end of the railcar. Mr. Cole had lost his hat. Billy saw blood on his forehead. But at least he was alive! Mr. Mackey and Philip had managed to hang on, too.

"Mike?" Billy called. "Mr. Elliston?"

"And keep your eyes open for men from the mucking crew," Mr. Cole said. "The water could have swept them up and carried them our way."

Billy saw the engineer, pressed up against one side of the locomotive engine. He was trying to avoid the water gushing in through the windows. But where were Mike and Ross?

Then Billy heard a sputtering noise.

"Over here!" Mike's shaky voice called out. "I think Mr. Elliston is hurt!"

The water wasn't moving quite so strongly or loudly now. Billy, his father, and Mr. Mackey were able to help Mike and Mr. Elliston back into the railcar. It was still leaning at an angle against the tunnel wall. Philip sat huddled on one of the tilted seats, shivering. The water around him was waist high. Ross sat down heavily next to him.

"Ohhhh!" he groaned, clutching his ankle. His face was twisted in pain.

Billy's father gingerly lifted Mr. Elliston's sopping pants leg. "Looks like it's broken," he said. "We'd better get you to the hospital."

* * *

"How's Mr. Elliston, Dad?"

Billy jumped up from the bench where he and Philip had been sitting in the front room of the hospital. Nurse Jeffers, the camp nurse, had seen to their scrapes. She had given them each a blanket, but wouldn't allow them into the sick ward.

"His ankle's broken, but he'll be fine," Mr. Cole

said. A bandage was taped across his forehead. He raised an eyebrow at Billy's wet, muddy clothes.

"Those boys flat out refused to go home and change, Mr. Cole," Nurse Jeffers said. "Said they won't budge 'til they see for themselves Mr. Elliston is all right."

Billy didn't bother to look at Philip. The two of them had hardly spoken a word to each other while they waited. Billy knew that if he opened his mouth, he would tell Philip exactly what he thought of him. It was Philip's fault Finn's uncle was hurt. What kind of crazy fool jumped off a train in the middle of a tunnel?

For once, Philip didn't seem to have a thing to say. He sat as silent as a stone.

"Well, I guess you can see him. But just for a minute," Billy's father said. "Your mother is talking to the families of the injured men. She wants me to get you home right away."

The two boys left their blankets on the bench. Mr. Cole led them into the sick ward. It was a large room. A dozen beds were lined up against the walls. Billy could see bandages and medical instruments through the glass doors of a cabinet.

Mr. Elliston lay on the bed closest to the door. His left foot was propped up on pillows. A plaster cast surrounded his ankle and foot, so that just his toes stuck out.

Mike Renwick sat on the next bed over. His shirt was off, and he held a bag of ice to his shoulder. Mr. Mackey and the engineer of the work train stood nearby. As far as Billy could tell, they had no injuries.

Two workers from the tunnel hadn't been so lucky. They had been brought in on stretchers. Nurse Jeffers told Billy and Philip that the men had been working the mucking machines inside the tunnel. Water had burst through the newly blasted rock right next to them. Both men lay in bed now. Their heads and chests were heavily bandaged.

Mr. Elliston smiled when he saw Billy and Philip. "Dr. Riley tells me I'll be visiting Scenic a day or two longer than I expected," he said. He nodded at a balding man in a white coat who was bent over one of the other patients. Then Finn's uncle looked expectantly past Billy, at the doorway.

"I've sent word to your sister," Mr. Cole said. "I expect she'll be here soon."

Billy sure hoped so. Mr. Elliston needed family, now that he was hurt.

"Um, Mr. Elliston?" said Philip. He shifted from foot to foot. For a moment, Billy thought he might apologize for jumping down on the tracks. But the railroad owner's son scowled and pointed at Mike.

"It was all *his* fault!" Philip said.

Mike had put down the ice and was pulling on his shirt. He glanced impatiently at Philip. "Oh yeah? What did *I* do?" he said.

"Isn't it your job to keep things secure?" Philip said.

"This young man did a fine job," Mr. Mackey said.

"And he got hurt saving *you!*" Billy added. *"You're* the one who didn't do what you were supposed to!"

"Enough bickering," Mr. Cole said. He looked sharply at Billy. "Boys, I need you to do an errand for Mr. Elliston. You'll have to use the telephone in my office to ring up the other pilots from the air show. They're staying at the hotel in Skykomish."

Mr. Elliston winced as he sat up in bed. "We've got a show down in Oregon in two days. You tell Mabel and Dan to fly there without me," he said. "I hate to miss a show. But I can't fly 'til this ankle mends some."

"Don't you worry, Mr. Elliston. We'll tell them," Billy promised.

There were just two telephones in all of Scenic. One was in the security office. The other sat on the desk in Mr. Cole's office. Billy had used it only once before.

"Let me do the talking," Philip said.

"No," Billy said firmly. "I know how to handle this."

Philip sulked. But when Billy got on the line and Ida Hawkins, the operator, pelted him with her usual nosy questions, Billy was ready.

"It's a broken ankle, Mrs. Hawkins," he told her. "The doctor says Mr. Elliston will be able to get around in a few days.... What? Mr. Mackey? Yes, he was there, but he's all right.... Yes ma'am, there were other injuries. No, I don't know their names, but they're in the hospital."

"You don't say!" the operator said, for the tenth time.

It seemed like forever before Mrs. Hawkins was satisfied with every detail Billy gave her. Only then did she put his call through to the hotel. Billy waited, shivering in his damp clothes, until a woman's voice crackled over the line. It was Mabel Otis, one of the pilots. Billy explained what had happened.

"Broken, eh?" Mabel whistled. "Well, that explains where Ross has been all day. Dan and I were wondering. You tell Ross not to worry. We can handle the show. Oh—and tell him some folks have been around, asking for him."

Billy squeezed the handset of the telephone more tightly. "What kind of folks? What did they look like?" he asked.

"What did who look like?" Philip said loudly, right in Billy's ear.

"Shhh!" Billy told him. But it was too late. He had already missed Mabel's answer.

"And tell Ross to get down to Oregon as soon as he's able," Mabel said. "Bye, now!"

She rang off, and the line went dead.

Billy put the handset back in its cradle on top of the phone. Stop worrying, he told himself. An interesting man like Mr. Elliston probably knew loads of folks. There was no reason to think the men looking for him were the ones he and Finn had seen at the air show.

As he and Philip stepped out of the lodge, Billy saw Finn and Dannie. His friends were hurrying along the road toward the hospital. With them was Finn's mother.

"We just heard!" Dannie called. "Mike told us what happened."

"Trouble sure does seem to follow Ross," Mrs. Mackenzie said with a sigh.

"Mother!" Finn said. "It wasn't Uncle Ross's fault. Water burst through the tunnel all on its own. He didn't have a thing to do with it!"

"That's right," Billy added. "If it wasn't for Mr. Elliston and Mike, Philip might have been killed!"

Philip kicked at the gravel while Billy told the whole story.

"See?" Finn said to his mother. "It's just like I said. Uncle Ross is different now. He is a hero."

"Well, maybe so," Finn's mother said. Her voice was filled with doubt. She twisted the edge of her sweater between her fingers. "But the Ross I grew up with used to get into every kind of bad mess. Cheating, fist fights.... When he ran off to the war, it wasn't to be a hero. It was because he got himself into such trouble that he had to get out of town!"

Finn, Billy, and Dannie all stared at each other. "What did he do?" Finn asked.

Mrs. Mackenzie shook her head. "It hardly matters now," she said. "Maybe Ross has changed. But I'm not sure a leopard can change its spots."

"Uncle Ross put himself in danger to save Philip!" said Finn. "He didn't have to do it. But he did!"

"So did my brother," Dannie added.

Philip jammed his hands in the pockets of his wet, muddy sailor suit. "It wasn't my fault," he muttered. He walked quickly down the road.

The others hurried after him. They passed the Model T Billy's father kept parked next to the lodge. Just ahead was the hospital.

They were still several yards away when a loud crash made them stop short. It sounded to Billy as if something had clattered to the floor inside the hospital. A cry of pain pierced the air.

"Ross?" Mrs. Mackenzie said. The doubt vanished from her face, and worry took its place. She ran through the hospital door.

Billy and the others were right behind her. They raced through the waiting room to the sick ward.

"Hey! What's going on?" Billy said. He skidded to a stop just inside the door.

Two men were pulling Mr. Elliston roughly from his bed. A chair lay overturned on the floor next to them. Finn's uncle was breathing hard.

"What are you kids doing here?" he said. For the first time since Billy had seen him, the daredevil pilot seemed afraid.

Then one of the men turned around. His beady eyes made Billy's blood run cold.

Chapter Eight

STRANGERS IN SCENIC

M r. Elliston!" Billy cried.

He looked wildly around the sick ward. The only other people in the room besides the strange men were the two heavily bandaged patients.

Where have Dr. Riley and Nurse Jeffers gone? Billy wondered.

"What's the meaning of this?" said Finn's mother. If she was scared of the two men, she didn't show it. She marched right over to them, her hands on her hips.

"You get your hands off my uncle!" Finn added. He ran to join his mother. Billy, Dannie, and Philip followed right behind them.

The two men stopped. Mr. Elliston was still sandwiched between them. He saw Finn's mother, and his face went pale.

"Rose?" he said weakly. He looked as if he had seen a ghost. But Billy saw a glimmer of hope, too.

Finn's mother nodded. Tears shone in her eyes. She wiped them away, then turned back to the men who held Mr. Ross.

"I don't know who you think you are," she said. "But my brother is in no condition to be moved!"

The shorter man shifted his beady eyes from Mrs. Mackenzie to the children. He nodded at the larger man, and they let go of Mr. Elliston. Finn's uncle swayed on his good leg.

"Ross!" Finn's mother hurried to help him back to his bed.

"Er…excuse me, ma'am," said the man with the beady eyes. He took off his hat. "I'm Mr. Smith. Joseph Smith. My friend and I have some business with Mr. Elliston."

Billy recognized the man's rasping voice. It was the same one he and Finn had heard threatening Ross at the air show.

"We know the kind of business you're mixed up in. Smuggling bootleg liquor!" Dannie burst out.

Mrs. Mackenzie looked at Dannie in surprise. "Hush up, now. This is no matter for children," she told her. Then she turned to Ross.

"Bootleggers?" she said. Anger flashed in her eyes. "So that's the kind of folks you're associating with now?"

"It's not like that, Rose," Mr. Elliston began.

Finn's mother didn't give him a chance to explain. "Finn almost had me believing you were different now. But you haven't changed a bit. Not since you stole that money from Avery's store back in Cedar Plains!"

Billy gaped at Finn's uncle. So that was the awful thing he had done!

"I was young," Mr. Elliston said quickly. "Foolish. I'm not like that anymore, Rose. Truly, I'm not."

There was a pained look on Mrs. Mackenzie's face. It was as if she wanted to believe her brother—but wasn't sure she could.

"Isn't it bad enough you ran off to the war and left Mother and Father to pay back all the money?" she said. "Now you're getting our young Finn and his friends mixed up in your no-good business, too!"

"Uncle Ross *isn't* mixing with bootleggers!" Finn insisted. "They were trying to hurt him because he won't have any part of their smuggling!"

Billy nodded. "Mr. Elliston helps to put scoundrels like them in jail," he added. He turned to Finn's uncle. "Like those robbers in Kansas. Right, Mr. Elliston?"

"That's right," the pilot said. He looked Finn's mother right in the eye. "I can't stop you from believing the worst. But I have changed."

"I believe you, Uncle Ross," Finn said. He nodded toward the two strangers. "Do you want me to go get Mr. Jenkins from the security office?"

"No need, son. I can handle this," Mr. Elliston said.

The hospital door pushed open. Dr. Riley and Nurse Jeffers walked into the sick ward. Nurse Jeffers was balancing three trays of meat loaf and mashed potatoes with gravy.

"We've got a surprise for you, Mr. Elliston," the doctor said, smiling. "We got supper from the cookhouse just as you asked. But it looks like the ladies of Scenic thought some home cooking would be better medicine."

Dr. Riley stepped aside to make room for half a dozen ladies behind them. They all carried pans or plates of food. Miss Wrigley stood at the front of the group carrying an iced cake.

"Oh." Dr. Riley paused as his gaze landed on Mr. Smith and his companion. "Can I help you gentlemen?"

"These men stopped in for a surprise visit after you left. They're just leaving," Mr. Elliston said.

"Yeah," said Dannie. She turned to face the two

men. "Mr. Elliston doesn't want any part of your dumb bootlegging. So get out!"

Mr. Smith's beady eyes got even smaller. Billy heard him whisper, "Our business isn't finished, Elliston. Not by a long shot."

Then he and his companion walked out of the sick ward. A tense silence filled the room.

"Who *were* those men?" Alice Ann's mother said. She and the other ladies hurried to Mr. Elliston and the two other injured men. Questions flew around the sick ward.

"Bootleggers, here in Scenic? Honestly!"

"Whatever could they want with you, Mr. Elliston?"

"Mr. Elliston, would you like some cake?"

Billy, Finn, and Dannie walked over to the pilot's bedside. Mr. Elliston's face was pale. He barely managed a smile as Finn's mother and Miss Wrigley placed pillows behind his head and beneath his injured ankle.

"I never knew a little feminine touch could be so powerful," Mr. Elliston said, chuckling. "You ladies arrived in the nick of time. Even you, Rose."

Just then, Dannie's brother came skidding back into the sick ward. His shoulder seemed better. But one look at Mike's ashen face, and Billy knew something was very wrong.

"Billy, come quick," Mike said. "It's Philip!"

Billy glanced around the room. He hadn't even realized Philip was no longer with them.

"Where is he?" Billy asked.

"A couple of men drove off toward Skykomish," Mike said. "Philip went chasing down the road after them. But that's not the worst of it. Billy, he's driving your father's Model T!"

CHAPTER NINE

RUNAWAY AUTOMOBILE

"Philip's *driving?*" Dannie said, shocked.

Billy had never seen anyone their age drive an automobile. Some of the older boys, maybe. But only the ones who were tall enough to see past the hood of the car. Billy doubted Philip could see the road well enough to steer.

"Does Dad know?" he asked.

Mike shook his head. "He's inside the tunnel inspecting the water damage with Mr. Mackey," he said. "Cal's not here, either." Cal Jenkins was the chief of security in Scenic.

"Well, we'd better not wait for them," Billy said. "There's no time. Philip could drive off into a ditch. Maybe even have an accident!"

Mike, Finn, and Dannie ran outside with Billy. His

eyes flew to the spot next to the depot, where he had last seen his father's Model T. Sure enough, it was gone.

"This way!" Mike said. He ran west along the road and cut through the woods.

Ahead, Billy could just see the boxy shape of his father's sedan. It was approaching the next hairpin curve. The ground dropped off sharply next to the road. Billy's heart lurched as the automobile suddenly swerved.

The Model T skidded dangerously close to the edge before finding the road again. Then it puttered out of sight behind the thick evergreens.

Billy kept running as fast as he could. It was beginning to get dark. "I'm going to pound that Philip," he said.

"If you don't, I will," Finn puffed from behind him.

Dannie and Mike were just ahead of them. There was a loud bang of a backfiring engine, and half a dozen black swifts fluttered up from the trees. Then came the screech of tires.

"Oh, no!" Dannie shouted. She, Billy, Mike, and Finn flew forward on the darkening road. Their boots sent up a spray of gravel. Billy's chest heaved. His breath seemed to scrape against the shadows as he ran.

"There!" Mike said.

Billy peered into the darkness. At last he saw his father's sedan again. It had skidded sidewise and sat half off the road. Philip was behind the wheel.

A wave of relief washed over Billy. Philip wasn't hurt.

The railroad owner's son was muttering under his breath. He pulled levers and pumped at the pedals on the floor of the Model T. The engine made a sick chugging noise, then fell silent.

Billy flung open the door and yanked Philip out by his muddy sailor collar. "Are you crazy?" he said. Philip landed hard on the gravel, but Billy didn't care. "That's Dad's Model T! You can't just drive off in it. Do you know what kind of hot water I'll be in if Dad finds out?"

"Help me get it started," said Philip. He scrambled to his feet and reached for the door. Mike, Finn, and Dannie blocked his way.

"We can't let you do that," Mike said firmly. "Anyone can see you don't know much about driving. Anyhow, don't you know chasing after smugglers is dangerous?"

The road was almost completely hidden in shadows now. A mountain lion howled somewhere high up the mountainside. Philip bit his lip, staring up at the dark mass of fir trees.

"I-I know what I'm doing," he said. He stomped his muddy shoe on the road. "Father lets me drive his

Bentley whenever I want. He'll be plenty steamed when he finds out you stopped me." He glared at Mike.

Mike didn't answer. His jaw was tight as he climbed behind the wheel of the Model T. He fiddled with the gas lever, choke rod, and clutch pedal. The engine chugged, then started up.

"Let's get back to camp," he said.

* * *

"Why do *they* have to be here?" Dannie muttered later that evening.

She, Billy, and Finn were sprawled on the rug in Billy's cabin. Dannie nodded at Philip and Alice Ann. They sat right next to the radio in the only two chairs.

"Mother made me invite Philip for *Sam 'n Henry*," Billy whispered. "Then he went and told Alice Ann she could come, too."

Dannie and Finn came to Billy's house most evenings to hear their favorite radio show. Somehow, it just wasn't the same with Philip and Alice Ann there.

"I met the real Sam 'n Henry, you know," Philip was saying. He puffed out his chest. "Father hired them for my birthday this year."

Of course Alice Ann oohed and aahed at whatever

Philip said. Between the two of them, no one could hear a word of *Sam 'n Henry.*

Billy took a deep breath. "Finn, are you afraid those two hoodlums might come back and try to hurt your uncle again?"

"Well, sure," Finn said. "Mother is, too. She made Cal Jenkins promise to spend the night at the hospital."

Dannie raised an eyebrow at Finn. "So she's ready to believe he's not such a bad sort anymore?"

"Well, Mother still thinks what he did back in Cedar Plains was awful," Finn said. "But she had to admit saving Philip in the tunnel was brave. And Uncle Ross sure stood up to those bootleg smugglers. Mother says maybe he deserves a second chance after all."

Billy was glad about that. But he couldn't shake off the uneasy feeling that had settled in his own gut.

"How do you suppose those men found your uncle?" he asked. "Mabel Otis and that other pilot didn't even know he was here."

"Someone else must have known," Dannie said, shrugging.

"Maybe," said Billy. "But who?"

He thought about that question even after everyone else went home.

But, try as he might, he couldn't think of an answer.

CHAPTER TEN

TEMPERS AND TROUBLE

Whispers flew around Miss Wrigley's class the next morning. Everyone wanted to hear about the accident inside the tunnel. Boys and girls pelted Finn with questions about his uncle, too. Had hoodlums really tried to hurt him? Bootleggers?

"Eyes on your lessons, children!" Miss Wrigley said. But even her sternest scolding couldn't stop the buzz of voices. A few times, Billy even caught her listening.

"Look at Philip," Dannie said, nudging Billy.

Philip sat at the end of the fourth-grade row. He stared stonily down at his grammar text. Billy thought he knew why.

"Every time someone asks about the accident, Finn tells how his uncle got hurt saving Philip," Billy whispered back. "Now everyone knows what a dumb thing Philip did."

Philip's cheeks got redder with each telling of the story. When the noon hour came, he was quick to escape. He grabbed his lunch pail from the coatroom and ran outside.

"Philip, wait!" Alice Ann called. She, Lucy, and Janet pushed past Billy and hurried over to him. The girls and Philip walked toward a sunny spot near the Tye. They didn't seem to notice Billy and his friends behind them.

"Mr. Elliston says I was the real hero when the water hit," Philip was saying.

"How does he figure *that?*" Finn whispered to Billy.

"Water was everywhere, but I kept my head," Philip went on. "I'm the one who made sure Mr. Elliston and Mike got back on the railcar safely."

Billy frowned. Philip was making up every word of his story!

"Soon as I saw Mr. Elliston's ankle, I knew it was broken," Philip bragged. "Everyone else was too scared to move. But I said straight away we had to get him to the hospital."

"That's a lie!" Dannie burst out loudly. *"You're* the one who was scared. My brother and Mr. Elliston made sure *you* got back on the car!"

Philip turned and glared at her. "If he had been doing his job right…"

Dannie shoved both hands into Philip's chest, hard. He stumbled down the bank in his short pants and jacket. He managed to stop himself just short of the water.

"Ha! You couldn't even get me in," Philip said.

The prickly feeling at the back of Billy's neck turned into red-hot anger.

"Well, *I* can," Billy said. He didn't care what his father might say.

Dropping his lunch pail, he ran down the bank toward Philip. He pushed him, and Philip flew backward. He landed on his backside in the Tye River.

"That's what you get for lying!" Billy told him.

Alice Ann shouted something, but Billy paid no attention. "It's your fault Mr. Elliston broke his ankle in the first place!" he added.

"Is not!" Philip retorted. He tried to get up. But his feet slipped over the rocky riverbed.

Billy ignored the voice at the back of his head that told him he should help. Instead, he pushed Philip deeper into the river. He couldn't stop the angry words that flew from his mouth.

"You're *not* a hero. You're the worst kind of coward—and a spoiled troublemaker to boot. I wish you'd never come to Scenic!" Billy yelled.

All at once, he realized that everyone around him and Philip had fallen silent. He turned and saw Miss Wrigley at the top of the bank. She glared down at Billy, her hands on her hips.

"Billy Cole!" she scolded. "You will spend the rest of lunch inside. *After* you help Philip out of that water."

"Dannie started it," Alice Ann piped up. "She pushed Philip first."

"Oh?" Their teacher turned her cool gaze to Dannie. "Daniella, you will join Billy," she said. Then, in a kinder voice, she added, "Philip, why don't you run to the lodge and change? There's plenty of time before afternoon lessons begin."

Billy reluctantly held out a hand toward Philip. Philip swatted it away. "I don't need your kind of help," he sputtered. "And I'm not a coward. You'll see. I'll show you all!"

Billy shrugged and waded out of the stream. He tried to ignore Miss Wrigley's disapproving gaze.

Inside the classroom, he and Dannie ate in silence. Billy knew they had a lecture coming. But before Miss Wrigley could give it, Mr. Farnam appeared in the classroom doorway.

"May I have a word with you, please?" he asked Miss Wrigley. He sounded more formal than usual—even a little cool. Miss Wrigley glanced at him in surprise.

"Of course," she said. Her shoes tapped against the floor as she joined Mr. Farnam in his empty classroom.

While Billy and Dannie ate, they listened to the teachers in the other room.

"You know, my brother Luke fought in the Great War," Mr. Farnam was saying.

"Really? Did he know Mr. Elliston?" Miss Wrigley asked.

There was a pause before Mr. Farnam answered. "As a matter of fact, he did. But…well, I'm afraid he doesn't recall Ross Elliston as much of a hero."

Dannie's eyebrows shot up. "What's he trying to say?" she whispered.

Billy shrugged. He sat with his hard-boiled egg in midair. He didn't want to miss a word Mr. Farnam and Miss Wrigley said.

"The way Luke tells it, Ross was a coward," Mr. Farnam went on from the next room. "First time the fighting got bad, he turned tail in his plane. The men in his squadron never saw him again."

"I don't believe that for a minute," Dannie whispered to Billy.

Miss Wrigley seemed to share Dannie's reaction. "Ross Elliston is as brave as any man I have met," she said. Her voice sounded colder than the freezing waters of Surprise Lake, high up the mountain. "Why, I'm surprised that you would spread this sort of rumor, Mr. Farnam. Ross Elliston, a deserter? It simply is not possible."

There was a tense silence. Then Mr. Farnam said gruffly, "I thought you should know, that's all." Billy heard frustration in his voice. "Isn't it possible that...emotion is affecting your good sense?"

"Certainly not!" Miss Wrigley said. Billy heard the scrape of a chair. "Please do not mention this matter to me again, Mr. Farnam."

* * *

"He's jealous!" Finn said.

School had just ended for the day. Billy and Dannie tripped over each other's words in their hurry to tell Finn about the argument between the two teachers. Buster had been waiting for them outside the school-house. Now the retriever ran along the creek bank.

"That's what I think, too," Dannie said. She tossed a stick for Buster to catch. "Mr. Farnam can't stand that Miss Wrigley is sweet on Ross. I bet he made up that story."

It was true. Mr. Farnam had been unusually cool toward Ross. But Billy hated to think he would lie. And he couldn't think about that now. He had other things on his mind.

"You don't suppose that Mr. Smith and his pal came back, do you?" Billy said. "I know Mr. Jenkins promised to keep an eye on the hospital. But I just hope nothing bad happened."

"Well, Uncle Ross made me promise to come visit, soon as school was over. Let's all go," Finn said. "We can tell him how we got even with Philip."

Philip hadn't returned to school after lunch. Billy supposed he was too humiliated. He tried to push away the twinge of guilt in the back of his mind.

Philip got what he deserved, Billy thought.

He, Finn, and Dannie crossed the bridge to the main part of camp. They heard the whistle of the local train. By the time they reached the depot, the train was just leaving. It chugged away on its zigzag path up the mountain.

A lone passenger had gotten off. He stood on the depot platform, looking around. Billy could tell right away he wasn't a worker on any of the tunnel crews. This man wore a jacket and trousers, not the denim coverall used by most workers. He carried a leather case, too. Square glasses were perched on the man's hooked nose.

"Excuse me," the man said. "I'm looking for a fellow by the name of Elliston. Ross Elliston. Do you know where I might find him?"

One look at Finn and Dannie's shocked faces, and Billy knew what his friends were thinking.

Mr. Elliston had barely escaped being hurt by Mr. Smith and his hoodlum friend. Now someone *else* was after him!

Chapter Eleven
A Desperate Plan

Billy gulped. They had to keep this man from finding Finn's uncle!

"Mr. Elliston?" Finn said. He glanced nervously at the hospital. It was just up the road from the depot. "He's, um…"

Billy's eyes landed on Buster. The dog had trotted ahead. He was sniffing a noisy generator that sat outside the tunnel. It ran the pumps that sucked water from inside the mountain.

That's it! Billy thought.

A pipe ran from the tunnel to a gully just north of the tunnel entrance. Thousands of gallons of water had already been pumped out. Billy had seen the enormous, muddy swamp that had formed in the gully.

"I'll tell you exactly how to find Mr. Elliston, sir!" he

told the man with the glasses. "You can take a shortcut through a gully just past the tunnel entrance...."

When Billy was done, the man thanked him. Billy chuckled as the man walked past the hospital and toward the tunnel.

"He'll be stuck in that mud for a week!" Dannie said.

"Well, Buster gave me the idea," Billy said. He watched Dannie's dog chase some squirrels into the trees. Then a movement at the depot caught his eye. Cal Jenkins was just stepping onto the platform from the lodge.

"Mr. Jenkins!" Dannie called. She, Billy, and Finn raced up the depot steps from the road. "There was a man here looking for Mr. Elliston."

Mr. Jenkins gave a nod. He didn't seem surprised.

"We think he wants to hurt him!" Billy added.

"We sure fooled him, though," said Finn. "Come on, let's go warn Uncle Ross!"

Finn tried to pull Mr. Jenkins toward the hospital. "Hold on a minute now. Let me get this straight," the head of security said. "Someone *else* is after Mr. Elliston? And what's this about fooling him?"

Finn, Dannie, and Billy all talked at once. Mr. Jenkins listened calmly—until they told him about the "short cut" they had made up to trick the man.

"Oh no!" Mr. Jenkins groaned. "Kids, that man is no gangster. Mr. Kresky rang me up himself to say he was coming. And now you've gone and sent him on a wild goose chase into that muddy mess."

"Who is Mr. Kresky?" Billy wanted to know.

Mr. Jenkins didn't answer. He was already hurrying down the depot steps. He disappeared down the road.

"How can Mr. Jenkins be so sure that man won't hurt Uncle Ross?" Finn said. "I still think we've got to warn him."

Finn didn't bother with the steps. He jumped right down off the platform. By the time Billy and Dannie caught up to him, he was pulling open the hospital door.

Finn stopped short in front of Billy.

"What's the matter?" Billy asked.

Mike Renwick blocked their way into the front room. His arms were folded in front of his chest. His SECURITY band was pinned to his sleeve.

"Sorry, I can't let you kids in," Mike said firmly.

"But I'm your sister," said Dannie. "You can let me in."

"Nope. Not even you."

"Why not?" Dannie asked.

"Mr. Jenkins's orders," Mike said. "I'm not to let

anyone in but Dr. Riley and Nurse Jeffers," he said. "Or I'll lose my job."

Billy knew Dannie's family needed every penny Mike could earn. They were still paying off debts from taking care of Dannie's mother before she died. But…

"We got to see him yesterday," Billy said. "Why not today?"

"Did something happen to Uncle Ross?" Finn asked, sounding worried.

"No. There hasn't been any more trouble," Mike told him.

Billy looked past Mike. He heard voices inside. Someone was talking to Mr. Elliston. Someone whose snooty voice Billy recognized right away.

"Hey, Philip's in there!" he said. "How come *he* gets to see Mr. Elliston, and we don't?"

"Mr. Mackey said it was all right. I couldn't say no to the boss, could I?" Mike said in a low voice.

"All right," Dannie said. "But you'd better warn Mr. Elliston that trouble's coming."

They told him about the man with the glasses. But Mike still wouldn't let them in. After promising to tell Mr. Elliston, Mike shooed them away.

Billy and his friends stood in front of the hospital, wondering what to do next. "Gee whiz!" Finn said.

"Uncle Ross could be in big trouble. And we can't even talk to him!"

"Well, I know something we *can* do," Dannie said. She started down the gravel road toward the tunnel.

"What?" Billy asked.

Dannie's dark eyes sparkled with challenge. "We can find out exactly who Mr. Kresky is," she said. "And what business he has with Finn's uncle."

* * *

"There they are!" Finn whispered.

He, Dannie, and Billy had crept into the woods just north of the tunnel entrance. They crouched behind a fir tree at the top of a gully. A metal pipe ran along the ground next to them. A steady stream of water spilled from the end of the pipe. It ran down the steep slope into the wet gully beyond.

Billy almost laughed when he saw Cal Jenkins and the man with the glasses. They stood knee-deep in the thick, brown ooze. Mr. Kresky was completely coated in dripping mud. Billy saw marks where he had slipped on the wet slope.

"My papers could be ruined," Mr. Kresky was saying. He and Mr. Jenkins both held long sticks. They dragged them through the mud, as if they were searching for something. Each time one of them took a step, the mud made loud, sucking noises. "All the evidence will be lost."

Mr. Kresky was no longer holding his worn leather case, Billy saw. That had to be what the men were looking for. But it was his words that stuck in Billy's mind.

Papers? Evidence? What was Mr. Kresky talking about?

"Those darned kids," Mr. Jenkins muttered. He poked at the mud with his stick. "They have no idea you're a federal agent, Mr. Kresky."

Billy gaped at Finn and Dannie. *A federal agent!* What could someone like that want with Finn's uncle?

"Folks around here see Ross Elliston as a hero," Mr. Jenkins went on. "No one's going to want to hear he's been smuggling liquor in that Curtiss Jenny of his."

Finn's whole body stiffened. A scowl darkened his face. He looked as if he might storm down into the gully with his fists flying. Billy put a warning hand on his friend's shoulder.

"We weren't sure ourselves until after last week's raid," Mr. Kresky said. "We managed to put a few bullet holes in his wing during the chase. Of course, we didn't know then who was piloting that plane. One of my men spotted bullet holes in Elliston's wing at the air show in Skykomish."

Billy frowned. The newspaper hadn't said anything about airplanes in the raid. He had thought smugglers brought the bootleg liquor in by boat or truck.

He could still picture the gashes he had seen on the wings of Mr. Elliston's plane. Finn's uncle had said he'd gotten them while he was *helping* the police. Now, listening to Mr. Kresky, Billy wasn't sure.

Finn sat next to him. He was breathing hard and frowning.

"The funny thing is," Mr. Kresky continued, "the liquor doesn't seem to have been delivered. It hasn't turned up in any of the speakeasies we know in the state."

"Why in Sam Hill not?" Mr. Jenkins said. He rubbed his chin, smearing mud across it.

Mr. Kresky gave a shrug. "I figure Elliston hid it somewhere," he said. "He's probably staying low for a few days until things calm down."

Mr. Jenkins dragged his stick through the mud again. Suddenly, he reached down. There was a wet, sucking sound as he pulled something free of the ooze.

"Got it!" he said, holding up the dripping case.

"Good work, Jenkins," Mr. Kresky said.

The two men began to wade up and out of the gully. Billy, Finn, and Dannie tried to scramble away, but Mr. Jenkins spotted them.

"Hold it!" he growled. "Just what do you kids think you're up to, sneaking around like that?"

"Listening to a bunch of lies, that's what!" Finn shot back. He jabbed a finger at Mr. Kresky. "You don't know anything, mister. My uncle isn't running bootleg liquor in his plane. Those smugglers tried to hurt him, and he *still* wouldn't help them!"

"That so?" said Mr. Kresky. He was using his stick to scrape mud from his trousers and jacket. "Well, young man, there might be more to this than you know."

Finn opened his mouth again, but Mr. Jenkins held up a hand. "That's enough now. You kids stay out of this," he said.

Even so, Finn followed close at the men's heels as they headed back toward the road. Billy shrugged at Dannie, and they hurried to catch up.

Billy's mind raced. Nothing made sense anymore! Mr. Smith and his hoodlum partner *had* tried to hurt Ross. Surely, they wouldn't have done that if Mr. Elliston was helping them smuggle liquor. But Mr. Farnam had said that Finn's uncle wasn't the hero he made himself out to be. And now there was a federal agent after Mr. Elliston!

"At least now we can hear his side of the story," he whispered to Finn and Dannie. "If they let us into the hospital, that is."

Mr. Jenkins and Mr. Kresky stomped mud from their feet outside the hospital door. Mr. Jenkins opened the hospital door. "Mike?" he called.

He frowned slightly, stepping inside. "Mike!" he called again. "Dr. Riley? Nurse Jeffers?"

There was no answer.

Billy saw the grim look that shot between the two men. Mr. Kresky and Mr. Jenkins hurried toward the sick ward. They did nothing to stop Billy and his friends from following.

When they reached the doorway, Billy's eyes flew around the sick ward. There were just two patients in the room—the workers who had been injured inside the tunnel.

Mr. Elliston's bunk was empty.

"Jeepers," said Billy. "He's gone!"

Chapter Twelve

VANISHED!

B illy felt a twist in his gut. "How could Mr. Elliston be gone?" he said. "He can't even walk. His ankle is broken!"

Finn said nothing. He stared at the rumpled sheets on his uncle's empty bed.

"Mike's gone, too," Dannie added, frowning. "So are Dr. Riley and Nurse Jeffers."

"And Philip." Billy couldn't make sense of it. Where had they all gone? Was it just a coincidence that they had all left at once?

He glanced at the two injured men who remained in the ward. They wouldn't be much help. Both men were sleeping. Bandages covered their heads.

"I don't have time for this," Mr. Kresky muttered. His mouth pressed into a thin, angry line. "Every second we stand here, Elliston is getting farther away.

I've got to find him—before he delivers that cargo of bootleg liquor to Ribsy Smith's men!"

The federal agent's words seemed to snap Finn out of his silence. "Uncle Ross is no smuggler!" Finn insisted once again. "I bet anything that Mr. Smith came back—and his no-good friend, too. Only this time they got Uncle Ross!"

Cal Jenkins and Mr. Kresky exchanged skeptical glances. "Elliston must have convinced someone to drive him out of here," Mr. Jenkins said, without answering Finn. "There's still a chance we can catch them."

The two men were halfway to the door when it opened.

"Mike!" Dannie cried. "Where have you been? Where is Mr. Elliston?"

Mike was carrying a plate of fried chicken and mashed potatoes. He stared in surprise at everyone standing around him.

"He was here a minute ago," Mike said. "Asked for some supper. Doc Riley and Nurse Jeffers were called to the family cabins to deliver Mrs. Haverford's baby. So I went to the cookhouse for Mr. Elliston."

At that moment, something clicked in Billy's mind.

"The same thing happened yesterday!" he said.

"Remember when those two hoodlums came for Mr. Elliston? He asked Dr. Riley and Nurse Jeffers to go to the cookhouse then, too."

"You mean…you think he did it on purpose?" Dannie said.

Billy took a deep breath. He knew Finn wasn't going to like what he had to say. But the more he thought about it, the more it made sense.

"Well, what if that Mr. Smith and his partner *didn't* come here to hurt Mr. Elliston," Billy said. "What if they came to help him leave, so he could deliver the shipment of bootleg liquor to them?"

"You take that back, Billy!" Finn said angrily.

But Billy couldn't. "We all showed up before Mr. Elliston could get away," he went on, thinking back. "We thought those men were hurting him. Maybe he decided to play along with the story, so we wouldn't know what was *really* going on."

Mike let out a low whistle. "Only he still needed to get out of Scenic. So when Dr. Riley and Nurse Jeffers were called away, he hoodwinked me into leaving him alone. And now he's gone!"

Mr. Kresky and Mr. Jenkins were already striding toward the door in their muddy clothes. "My automobile is outside the security office," Mr. Jenkins said.

The door banged shut behind them. In the silence that followed, Billy turned to look at Finn.

His friend's face was red. Angry lines cut across his brow. His hands were clenched into fists.

"YOU...TAKE...BACK...WHAT...YOU...SAID, BILLY COLE!" Finn screamed.

He leaped at Billy, knocking him down. He hammered on Billy's chest with his fists. "Uncle Ross *isn't* a smuggler. He's a hero! You said so yourself."

Billy tried to wriggle free. Gasping, he threw his hands up and shoved Finn backward. Dannie and Mike held Finn back, and Billy scrambled to his feet.

"We thought he was a hero," Dannie said. "But think about it, Finn. If your uncle was honest, would he leave without so much as a word to you? Or to your mother?"

Finn was breathing hard. The scowl never left his face. "Mr. Smith's men came to get him. I know they did," he insisted. "Uncle Ross could be hurt. Or even..."

"Those men are the kind folks notice," Billy cut in. "Someone would have seen them."

"What about Philip?" Finn asked. He whirled around to look at Mike. "Wasn't he here?"

"He left right before I went to the cookhouse," Mike

answered, shaking his head. "Said something about a special favor for Mr. Elliston."

"Maybe that was just Mr. Elliston's way of getting rid of Philip," Dannie suggested. "Philip might have seen something."

Billy groaned. So far, the railroad owner's son had caused nothing but trouble in Scenic. Still, Philip *had* been with Mr. Elliston right before Finn's uncle disappeared from the hospital.

"Guess it can't hurt to talk to him," Billy sighed.

He, Dannie, and Finn ran quickly to the lodge. The rambling old building held the barbershop, store, post office, and security office on its first floor. Billy knew that Philip and Mr. Mackey had rooms on the second floor, near Billy's father's office.

"Your father's not here, Billy!" a voice called out from the store, as the three of them raced past.

Billy paused to see Ernie Oliver, the young man who ran the store. "He and Mr. Mackey have been inside the tunnel all afternoon," Ernie said.

"We're not here to see Dad," Billy said. "It's Philip we're after."

"Oh, he's not here, either," Ernie said good-naturedly. "Drove off in that Model T your father keeps out front."

Billy stopped so suddenly that Dannie and Finn rammed into him from behind. "What!" he cried.

"Not again," Dannie groaned.

"Thought it was odd myself," Ernie said, rubbing his chin. He leaned against a counter that held everything from cigarettes to oilskin jackets. "But he had that pilot fellow with him, so I figured maybe your father said it was all right."

Billy felt his chest tighten. He could barely breathe. It was as if Ernie's words had sucked the oxygen right out of the air.

"Jeepers!" he squeaked out. "It's not all right, Mr. Oliver. It's *not* all right at all!"

Chapter Thirteen

DANGER ON THE MOUNTAIN

M aybe you were right, Billy," Finn said slowly. "I guess Uncle Ross did get Philip to drive him out of here. Does that make him a kidnapper, too?" His voice was shaking.

"Dunno," Billy said quietly.

"And what if Uncle Ross did smuggle bootleg liquor in his plane?" Finn added. "Philip could be driving him right now so he can give the liquor to Mr. Smith!"

Billy shuddered, thinking of Philip all alone with a bunch of bootleggers. "Philip could be in big trouble," he said.

"Well, shouldn't we *do* something?" Dannie said. "We've got to warn Mr. Jenkins and Mr. Kresky that Philip is there, too. I mean, Mr. Kresky is a federal agent. What if he has a gun?"

Finn nodded. "There are always a few automobiles in

that garage next to the machine shop," he said. "You know the one—where they sharpen the drills."

"Sure!" Dannie agreed. Her eyes lit up. "And Mike knows how to run an automobile."

"Now, hold on…" Ernie began.

But Billy, Dannie, and Finn were already out the door.

* * *

The three of them were waiting next to the depot when Mike drove up in a mud-splattered roadster a few minutes later. Billy and Finn squeezed into the narrow bench seat in back. The motor idled noisily. As soon as Dannie climbed in front next to Mike, Buster came bounding out of the trees. He barked and jumped up next to the car. His muddy paws rested on top of the door.

"Stay, Buster," Dannie told him. "Don't worry, boy. We'll be back as quick as we can."

With that, the roadster jerked forward. The sudden movement sent Billy flying against the seat back.

"Ow!" he said, feeling something hard behind him. He reached back and pulled out a mud-covered leather case. "Mr. Kresky's?" he said.

"Yep," Mike replied. He kept his eyes on the sharply curving road. His hands and feet worked the floor pedals and brake. "He left it in the hospital. I figured we should give it back—if ever we catch up to him and Mr. Jenkins."

Billy placed the muddy case on the bench between him and Finn. Finn picked it up and opened it.

"Finn! That's Mr. Kresky's own private property!" Dannie frowned at him over her shoulder.

Finn shrugged. "Well, if there's anything in here about Uncle Ross, I've got a right to see it," he said.

Dannie looked doubtful. But Billy agreed with his friend. He leaned forward, staring through the windshield of the roadster.

The sun was already low in the sky. The glaring light hit all of them full in the face. Mike squinted, muttering under his breath. Then the roadster puttered around a curve, into the shadows of the fir trees that grew thick on either side of the road.

"How far ahead do you think they are?" Dannie asked.

Her brother shrugged. "Dunno." The gravel road sloped sharply down the mountainside. Two black-tailed deer bounded across the road. The *rat-a-tat-tat* of a woodpecker echoed in the air. But there was no sign of any other car.

Central Islip Public Library
33 Hawthorne Avenue
Central Islip, NY 11722

"Rats," Finn mumbled. "How could Mr. Kresky call this evidence? It's just a bunch of scribble!"

He sat hunched over next to Billy. He was scowling down at some damp papers in his hands. Finn thrust them at Billy, then reached into the case for another handful.

"Careful!' Billy said as the papers fluttered toward the open window. He managed to grab them just before they flew out. Handwritten notes were scribbled across them. "Looks like some kind of report about the stuff that was smuggled. Twenty cases of whiskey from some Canadian company called Tolliver."

Whoever wrote the notes had also made a simple drawing of the Tolliver whiskey label. It showed a white triangle inside a black circle. A "T" was stamped in the middle of the triangle.

"Hey!" Billy said. "I've seen that mark before!"

"Yeah?" Finn said. He was busy looking at a new batch of papers.

"Remember when we went flying with your uncle? We were so high up we could see everything. Well, there were some crates in the woods near the railroad tracks. They had that same mark on them!"

"Huh." Finn stopped digging inside the leather bag. He stared at Billy from beneath his mop of wild, red hair. "Do you think it was that smuggled whiskey?"

Dannie spun around from the front seat. "I reckon so!" she said. "That must be where Mr. Elliston and Philip are headed. Go faster, Mike! We've got to catch up to Mr. Kresky and tell him."

Billy gulped as the roadster skidded around a sharp curve. A steep hill sloped sharply down from the edge of the road. The roadster hit a rock, just inches from where the ground dropped off. The car lurched, and Billy felt his heart leap into his throat. He tried not to look at the tangle of branches, logs, and scrub in the ravine below.

"Criminy, Mike!" he said. "Not *that* fast. We don't want to—"

At that moment Billy caught sight of something shiny and black at the bottom of the ravine.

"Mike, stop! There's a car down there!" he yelled.

Mike slammed his boot against the brake pedal. The roadster stopped with a sudden jerk. The engine stalled out, and a sudden silence surrounded them.

"A car?" Mike whipped his head left and right. "Where?"

Billy jumped out of the roadster. He peered down into the ravine.

"There! See it?" he said, pointing.

Half a dozen dead fir trees lay in a jumbled pile at the bottom of the ravine. Sticking out of the tangle of dried branches was the black sedan. Billy gulped when he saw that one whole side of the car was crumpled.

Then he spotted something else. Something that made a shiver run through him from head to toe.

"Philip," he said.

The railroad owner's son lay sprawled on the ground next to the sedan. His right arm was twisted unnaturally beneath him. There was a dark stain on the back of his sailor shirt.

"Philip!" Billy said again, shouting this time.

A flock of juncos objected to the noise, trilling from the trees above.

Not Philip. He lay on the ground without moving or making a sound.

Chapter Fourteen

HEROES

"Oh, no. Oh, no. Oh, no," Billy said.

He was already skidding down the steep slope toward Philip. Rocks and dirt flew out from under his feet. Branches snapped and slapped against his face and arms. Billy paid no mind. He heard the others crashing down the slope, too. But he didn't turn to look at them. His eyes were glued on Philip.

Please be all right, he begged silently. *Please be alive.*

Billy kept hoping Philip would respond in some way to the racket they were making. But Philip didn't budge. It seemed like forever before they climbed over the last tree trunk to reach him.

Mike bent over Philip. "He's breathing," he said quickly. "Looks like his arm's broken, though."

"We've got to get him to the hospital!" Dannie said. She frowned at the blood that stained the back of Philip's shirt.

Billy started clearing a path through the dry branches. "Let's carry him up," he said to Finn. His friend was just behind him.

"But…" Finn paused. "Where's Uncle Ross?"

In his worry for Philip, Billy had forgotten about Finn's uncle. He whirled around and peered into the crumpled hulk of his father's Model T.

"He's not in there," Billy said, relieved that the pilot wasn't hurt. "But he couldn't have gotten far. Not with that bad ankle."

All of a sudden, Finn let out a shout. "Uncle Ross!"

He ran between two trees to his left. Then he headed up the ravine.

Billy spotted Mr. Elliston through the trees. The pilot was dragging himself up the steep slope on his belly. His cast scraped against the rocky ground.

"Uncle Ross!" Finn cried again. "Stop! We'll help you!"

Mr. Elliston barely glanced back at Finn. He continued on his path up the ravine, wincing with pain.

Billy ran after Finn. They struggled through the tangle of logs and branches. At last they caught up to

Mr. Elliston. There were scratches and cuts all over him. Blood trickled from a gash on his cheek. One eye was swollen shut. The injured man barely seemed to notice them. He only stopped when Finn sat down on the slope right in front of him.

"Did you do it?" Finn asked. He gasped for breath. "Did you...did you smuggle that whiskey in your plane for those no-good men?"

His uncle frowned and turned away. "It was business," he said finally. "No one else was supposed to get mixed up in it."

"Well, they did," Billy spoke up angrily. "Philip got mixed up in it when you talked him into driving my dad's car. You're just lucky he's still alive. You didn't even stay to help him!"

"I guess Mother was right about you after all," Finn said slowly. "I told her you were a hero. We tried to protect you from that Mr. Smith and his partner. And all along you were on *their* side. I bet those stories you told about being so brave during the war were lies, too!"

Mr. Elliston pushed himself up to a sitting position. His face was tired and tight with pain. Billy thought he saw something else, too. A glimmer of regret? He couldn't be sure.

"I figured there wasn't any harm in my own family thinking the best of me," Mr. Elliston said gruffly. "Guess I was wrong, huh?"

"I reckon so," said Finn.

He picked up a handful of pebbles. One by one, he threw them at a tree trunk that lay across their path. When he spoke again, his voice was full of resolve.

"Soon as we get Philip to the hospital, we're going to ring up the police in Skykomish," Finn said. "You're going to jail, Uncle Ross."

* * *

"Here come Scenic's youngest heroes," Mr. Mackey announced the next afternoon. "Hip, hip, hooray!"

Billy, Finn, and Dannie had just walked into the hospital. Billy hadn't expected to find so many people waiting for them. Alice Ann, Lucy, Janet, Wes, and most of their other classmates had crowded into the ward. Miss Wrigley, Mr. Farnam, and plenty of parents were there, too. Billy spotted his own mother and father, and Finn's. Mike stood near the door, wearing his SECURITY armband. Dannie's father, Billy knew, was on shift inside the tunnel.

"Hip, hip, hooray!" everyone cheered back.

Billy, Finn, and Dannie grinned at one another. Wes and a few other boys stepped aside to make room for them. It was only then that they were able to see Philip.

He lay in one of the beds wearing striped flannel pajama bottoms. Billy saw right away why he wasn't wearing the top. An enormous bandage covered Philip's side and back. A plaster cast covered his right forearm and most of his hand. His face was bruised and scratched.

"Um, how do you feel?" Billy asked, stopping next to the bed.

"All right, I guess." Philip's eyes flickered up at Billy, Finn, and Dannie. "Father told me you're the ones who found me," he mumbled. His voice was so low Billy could barely hear him.

"The ones who *saved* you, is more like it!" Mr. Mackey boomed. He stood on the other side of Philip's bed, beaming down at Billy, Finn, and Dannie.

"I, uh…thanks," Philip said.

Billy's mouth fell open. It was the first nice thing he had ever heard Philip say. Billy was so surprised he couldn't think of how to answer.

"We're glad you're going to be all right," Dannie said.

There was an uncomfortable silence. Then Mike

spoke up from the doorway. "Say! Did you hear? The Skykomish police rang up Mr. Jenkins," he said. "Told him they found that smuggled whiskey in the woods near the railroad. Right where Billy told 'em it would be."

That got everyone talking. The ward filled with excited voices. To Billy's relief, people stopped staring at him, Dannie, Finn, and Philip.

"They arrested that horrible Mr. Smith, too," Billy heard his mother say. "Once they talked to Mr. Elliston, they had all the information they needed to put those smugglers behind bars."

The room went quiet again.

"Oh!" Mrs. Cole added, with an uncomfortable glance at Finn's mother. "I am so sorry, Rose."

Billy didn't hear what Finn's mother said. But the sad smile on her face told Billy how she probably felt. Next to her, Miss Wrigley was chattering to Philip's father.

"Imagine!" his teacher was saying. "Philip wasn't the only one who was taken in by Mr. Elliston's lies. He had us all fooled." Billy saw her eyes flicker toward Mr. Farnam. "Well, perhaps not *all* of us," she added.

She excused herself and walked over to Mr. Farnam. "I do hope you'll tell me more about your cousin some day," Billy heard her say. "The one who flew in the Great War?"

A smile spread across Mr. Farnam's face. "Why, you just name the time," he told her. "Maybe some evening before the moving picture?"

"Knock-knock," Finn spoke up behind Billy.

Before Billy could answer, Philip spoke up from his bed.

"Who's there?" he asked.

Billy, Dannie, and Finn all stared at him.

"Well, who's there?" Philip said again.

Finn rubbed his chin. Finally, he said, "Weekend."

"Weekend who?" Philip asked.

"Weekend show you our fort up on Lookout Rock, soon as you're up and around again," Finn said, smiling. "If you want to see it, that is."

"Sure. I'd like that," Philip said. He didn't sound smug at all now. "I might need a pair of knickers, though. And maybe some of those high-cut boots like you and Billy wear."

"Well, Philip, what do you know?" Billy said, grinning. "There just might be hope for you after all!"

Author's Note

I got the idea for the *Cascade Mountain Railroad Mysteries* from a surprising place—a calendar! A few years ago, my uncle, David Conroy, made the calendar as a present for our family. It was all about the building of the Cascade Tunnel in the 1920s. My grandfather was the general manager in charge of the project. He took his family—my 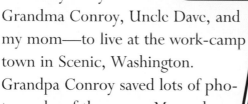 Grandma Conroy, Uncle Dave, and my mom—to live at the work-camp town in Scenic, Washington. Grandpa Conroy saved lots of photographs of the camp. My uncle used some of them in his calendar.

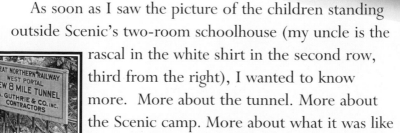

As soon as I saw the picture of the children standing outside Scenic's two-room schoolhouse (my uncle is the rascal in the white shirt in the second row, third from the right), I wanted to know more. More about the tunnel. More about the Scenic camp. More about what it was like to be a kid in Scenic back then. I started asking a lot of questions and doing research. The result is *The Cascade Mountain Railroad Mysteries.*

The Cascade Mountain Railroad Mysteries are made-up stories, but I've tried to make the setting as much like the real Scenic as possible. The bunkhouses, cookhouse, and family cabins were all part of the real camp. Silent movies were shown in the recreation hall, with one of the ladies playing piano accompaniment. Crystal Lake and the Tye River are also real. Other sites were invented for the story. I simplified descriptions of the tunnel to keep the story from getting too complicated. Also, I must admit that the map of the Scenic camp in this book is entirely made up! After three-quarters of a century, it is difficult to know exactly where everything was, but I have tried to capture the spirit of the place.

Why the Railroad Needed a Tunnel

Before the eight-mile Cascade Tunnel was built, crossing through the Cascade Mountains of Washington State was very dangerous, especially in the winter. Avalanches—giant snow slides—were a constant threat. To protect its passengers and trains, the Great Northern Railway built wooden shelters called snow sheds over the tracks. But the snow sheds weren't always enough. In 1910, an avalanche swept two trains off the tracks and 150 feet down into a canyon. 101 people were killed. Clearly, much better protection was needed.

Diagram of Cascade Tunnel route

Tunnels provided better shelter for the trains than snow sheds. A shorter tunnel, just 2.6 miles long, had already been built higher up the mountain. But the Great Northern Railway decided to build a new, longer tunnel lower down the mountainside, where snowslides were less of a danger. When the Cascade Tunnel was finished in 1929, it was the longest tunnel in the United States. It was called "a marvel of engineering skill" at the time it was built. At 8 miles, it is still one of the longest tunnels in the world today.

Daredevils of the Skies

1926 was an exciting time for the world of aviation. Pilots who had fought in The Great War, now known as World War I, were eager to keep flying. Many earned a living after the war by performing aerial tricks in their planes. These daring men and women traveled from town to town, putting on air shows wherever they went. They were called "barnstormers" because they often used a

Aerial combat in WWI

farmer's field or pasture for taking off and landing their planes.

Most barnstormers were thrill-seekers. They loved to perform stunts that were ever more exciting and dangerous: wing-walking, loop-the-loop, parachute drops, speed races. Sometimes they even changed planes in midair! And they did these stunts without any safety equipment at all.

Most barnstormers were known for their own special flying tricks. One pilot (who called herself "The Flying Witch") performed a stunt called the "Iron Jaw Spin." She dangled from an airplane by a rope that was clenched between her teeth! After twirling wildly in the air, she climbed back up the rope to the plane.

In those days, there were few rules to control what pilots could do. Many planes crashed. Pilots were injured and killed. But despite the dangers, men and women kept taking to the air. Some air shows were so big they were called "flying circuses." The Gates Flying Circus was the largest and most well-known flying circus. During the 1920s, pilots in the Gates Flying Circus gave rides to about 100,000 passengers a year.

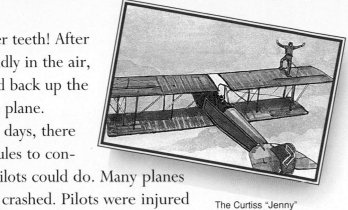

The Curtiss "Jenny" and a wingwalker

Poster advertising the famous Gates Flying Circus

Mabel Cody, niece of "Buffalo Bill" Cody, was a daring stuntwoman and skilled wingwalker.

The Dry 1920s

In 1920, a law called the National Prohibition Act was passed. Prohibition made it illegal to sell, make, or transport alcoholic beverages anywhere in the United States. The U.S. became a "dry" country.

Lawmakers hoped that if people stopped drinking there would be less crime, poverty, and poor health. But many people were determined to drink whether it was legal or not. A booming business of making and transporting illegal liquor began.

People who became involved with the illegal liquor business were called "bootleggers." The name dates back to colonial times, when the Georgia Colony outlawed alcohol. Despite the law, people continued to trade and drink liquor—hiding it inside their tall boots!

Jazz Age "flapper" hides a flask in her garter.

Bootlegging became a big business during Prohibition. People made their own alcohol, or smuggled liquor across the

A portable distillery, or "still," that people used for making "bathtub" gin.

border from Canada. Secret bars and taverns called *speakeasies* popped up all over the country. In 1926, the bootlegging business in the U.S. was worth over 4½ billion dollars! Organized gangs fought each other for control of bootlegging. The crime rate went *up* instead of down, especially in big cities.

There were so many bootleggers, and so many people who wanted to keep drinking, that government agents simply weren't able to stop them. In 1933, the law was finally taken away. Making, selling, and drinking alcohol for adults became legal once again.

In 1926...

■ World War I was still a recent memory. "The Great War," as it was called, had ended in 1919. During the war, biplanes such as the Curtiss "Jenny" and Sopwith Camel were used in battle for the first time. Ace pilots (men who had shot down at least five enemy aircraft) were hailed as bold and daring heroes when they returned home from Europe. Many of them loved the thrill of flying so much that they became barnstormers.

The Sopwith Camel

The Speakeasy. All people needed to get in was the password, the money, ...and the secret location!

■ Over 100 million gallons of bootleg liquor were sold in the United States. In New York City alone, there were over 100,000 speakeasies.

■ Commander Richard E. Byrd and Floyd Bennett became the first men to fly over the North Pole. (Charles Lindbergh would not make his historic flight across the Atlantic Ocean until 1927.)

■ The price of a daily newspaper was just two cents.

■ Children of the 1920s eagerly read the comic strips in the daily newspapers. Some of the most popular comics were Barney Google, Little Orphan Annie, Felix the Cat, Moon Mullins, and the Gumps.

A version of Felix the Cat in the 1920s